THE MAD
HERRINGTONS

THE MAD HERRINGTONS

•

Jane Myers Perrine

AVALON BOOKS
NEW YORK

© Copyright 2002 by Jane Myers Perrine
Library of Congress Catalog Card Number: 2002090084
ISBN 0-8034-9536-6
All rights reserved.
All the characters in this book are fictitious,
and any resemblance to actual persons,
living or dead, is purely coincidental.
Published by Thomas Bouregy & Co., Inc.
160 Madison Avenue, New York, NY 10016

PRINTED IN THE UNITED STATES OF AMERICA
ON ACID-FREE PAPER
BY HADDON CRAFTSMEN, BLOOMSBURG, PENNSYLVANIA

To George for his love and support

and to Kimberly Hammond, a beautiful redhead who left us far too soon.

Chapter One

The Mad Herringtons.

Blast them all! Aphrodite Herrington cursed to herself.

Through the swirling white of the debutantes' gowns and the deep blue of the coats worn by the gentlemen, in the light of hundreds of candles, Aphrodite could just catch a glimpse of her parents. She gazed at them for a moment, unable to tear her eyes from the glorious couple, then blushed and turned away.

At Almack's, the most exclusive assembly rooms in London, where the creme of society came to observe the mating ritual of the nobility, Aphrodite's father and mother, the Marquis and Marchioness of Temple, seduced each other in public while the *ton* danced and gaped. Polite society gaped politely, of course, behind fans and over padded shoulders, but, nonetheless, they gaped.

Aphrodite peeked over her shoulder and caught sight of her mother walking her slender white—and shockingly gloveless—fingers up the Marquis' neck and through his thick hair. The Marquis looked at his wife with a passion

1

usually reserved for a new *chère amie*, or so Aphrodite had heard.

"Isn't it romantic?" Athena, Aphrodite's younger sister, said with a sigh as their mother placed her other hand behind her husband's head and pulled his lips toward hers. "Oh, I want to find a man to love the way mama loves papa."

"I would think it excessively uncomfortable, not to mention demanding, unnatural, and exhausting." Aphrodite shifted her eyes toward her sister, who appeared lovely and innocent, an exterior which belied the underlying folly that infected the entire family—except Aphrodite herself. Athena's dark lashes fluttered over ethereally blue eyes and fanned translucent skin and pink cheeks. Then Athena's gaze crept around the room and pounced upon the Viscount Warwick.

Aphrodite's eyes followed Athena's glance to the viscount, heir to the Earl of Wharton. "No, Athena." She could read her younger sister's thoughts as if they were written across her alabaster forehead. Again, with the exception of Aphrodite, the Herringtons' faces conveyed every impression, every absurd idea that passed through their artless, passion-filled brains.

"He's so handsome, Ditie."

"Yes, I know," Aphrodite had to admit. Warwick was taller than any of the other men, his blue–black hair arranged fashionably around a face of such beauty that it was saved from being feminine only by a crooked nose and a pair of thick, dark eyebrows. When Warwick turned to speak to a friend, his muscular body showed through impeccable unmentionables and broad shoulders rippled under his perfectly fitted coat.

Aphrodite ruthlessly forced down a *frisson* that Warwick's appearance caused and said, "But he's not the man for you. He's a man of society, hardened. He wouldn't treat you the way you should be treated. He has other women . . ."

"Mistresses, Ditie?"

"Yes, dear."

The tears that gathered in Athena's eyes didn't mar her beauty. They made her eyes sparkle like diamonds shimmering through the clear blue water of a bottomless pond. "I wouldn't like for my husband to have a woman friend, other than me, or you, or perhaps Mama."

"You should be first in his heart, Athena," Aphrodite agreed. "You deserve that." She turned and searched the floor, delighted that her parents had waltzed from her sight and onto the balcony. Her eyes fell on the young sprig who came toward them. "Mr. Horne is an unexceptionable young man. Why don't you dance with him?"

"Ditie, I believe he wants to lead you out."

Indeed, the young man stopped before Aphrodite and bowed. "May I have this dance?"

"I am sorry, Mr. Horne. I do not dance the waltz, and Athena has not received approval from the patronesses to waltz."

"Please forgive me." The young man straightened and looked into Aphrodite's face. "Neither do I perform that scandalous dance. Please do not believe that I would ask a woman of such high standards to join me in flaunting good taste. A most wicked activity. I do not believe a woman of good reputation can be comfortable standing within a man's arm while others witness their intimacy."

"But Mama and Papa . . ." Athena began.

"Are married." Aphrodite completed the sentence.

"But the next is a country dance and the sets will be forming in a few minutes. If you would grant me the pleasure?"

"I would be delighted," Aphrodite said with a tilt of her head.

When the waltz ended, Mr. Horne led Aphrodite onto the floor. Although her partner had to concentrate on his steps, to the exclusion of conversation, she was pleased to find in the few sentences they exchanged that Mr. Horne was quite nice in his manners and that his beliefs were close to hers.

"It is a delight to meet a man so young but with his ideas so mature and well-founded," Aphrodite said as the dance ended and her partner escorted her to a chair.

"I owe it to my mother. A most unusual woman with great strength of character."

"I have not met her." Aphrodite settled herself on one of the gilded chairs, and Mr. Horne sat next to her. "Is she spending the season in London?"

"No, she hasn't visited here for many years. Her health has never been good but she insisted that I come for the season. I do return home to see her often. Not from duty, but because I have always found her to be the wisest of women."

"Oh, Mr. Horne, you are a good son."

"Thank you, my lady. That is not a quality admired by many of the *ton*."

"Those who judge by higher standards find love of parents a characteristic to respect."

"If you will excuse me?" A voice came from above the two. Aphrodite looked up to see Warwick. "May I have this dance, my lady?"

"As you can see, I am engaged in a conversation with Mr. Horne."

"Ah, but you can always converse with Horne." Warwick took Aphrodite's arm, lifted her from the chair, and led her onto the floor.

"That was highhanded," she complained as he began the steps of the dance.

"Certainly you didn't want to continue your conversation with Horne?"

"Should I not?" Aphrodite turned to the gentleman on her right and bowed.

"He's the most boring . . ." Aphrodite thought Warwick had said, but she wasn't sure, for the steps of the dance had taken him away from her.

"He believes just as he should," she said when Warwick returned to stand next to her.

He looked down at her, and his eyes held a look she couldn't decipher. His expression was not the warm one she had extinguished in other men with a few words spoken in a carefully modulated voice.

"You really do find Horne an interesting conversationalist?" he asked, his voice rising in disbelief.

Aphrodite turned away from him again as the dance required, then said when she was once again close enough, "Not exactly interesting but very well-mannered and *comme il faut*."

"Oh, yes, very *comme il faut*. You find that attractive in a man?"

"I would not expect you to understand, but it is enjoyable to talk to a man of sense," Aphrodite said as the steps of the dance parted them.

"Enjoyable?"

"And unusual. It's worthwhile to talk to a man of superior understanding."

"Understanding superior to whose?" Warwick said as he turned away from her and back.

Was he struggling not to laugh? Aphrodite wondered. His lips were quivering. Certainly not! Their conversation was hardly amusing, nor did people ever find what she said to be entertaining. "Superior to the conversation of the fribbles who inhabit these halls or who attend the balls and assemblies of the *ton*."

"Would you say most members of the *ton* are fribbles?"

"Of course not."

"Please excuse me, Lady Aphrodite, but I must ask. Are you really a Herrington?"

She stared at him, but the glare that had withered dozens of young men glanced off him. "Of course I am," she stated. "However, I am unlike the other Herringtons."

At that instant, her parents glided past her. They waltzed in spite of the fact that the orchestra played and the rest of the assembly danced to a country tune.

"I am different from the other Herringtons," she said, with conviction echoing in her voice.

"I thought so. With any other Herrington woman, if I were to whisper in her ear . . ." As he moved around her in step to the music, Warwick dropped his mouth to speak into what Aphrodite discovered was a most sensitive area. "If I were to whisper in the ear of one of your sisters, she would shiver delightfully."

Aphrodite turned away from the viscount, bit her lip, and took a deep breath. She forced herself to continue the steps of the dance, to keep her voice level, and not to display the shiver he had foretold, although the intimacy of Warwick's touch sent an amazing flutter through her entire body. She could only hope no one was aware of her heaving chest. "Indeed? And why is that?" she asked with remarkable control.

The movement of the dance occupied both until Aphrodite again took Warwick's arm. "Ah, because they are Mad Herringtons, ruled by passion. And you, of course, are not."

"I, clearly, am not."

After Warwick escorted her back to the gilded chairs, Aphrodite sought refuge in the retiring room. To the surprise of all the women who were there to repair a torn hem or smooth an unruly curl, she opened the window and leaned out, taking deep breaths and fanning herself.

"It is quite brisk for a spring day," one of the women stated but Aphrodite ignored her.

How does he do it? she wondered. How could a man touch a woman and leave her in such a dither? Her heart still hammered, and she knew her cheeks must be crimson—and fifteen minutes had passed. Oh, he was everything his reputation said. She doubted if any woman could withstand such an assault.

"What a fool you are," she whispered. "*You* can. You are not just any Herrington. You are Aphrodite Myrabella Herrington and can handle a host of Warwicks." With that, she closed the window, turned and strode toward the ballroom.

The next day, floral tributes came for Athena: posies from all the young men who had drowned in the depths of her eyes, the cards stated. As she opened them, Athena held them far away from her, leaning forward to sniff the blooms but careful not to allow any leaves to land on her embroidered morning gown of white lace with a rose underslip.

"I just wish these bouquets did not shed so," she complained as she brushed the offending petals from her lap.

For Aphrodite there were flowers sent by both Mr. Horne and Warwick. From Mr. Horne, there was a corsage of white carnations. Tasteful and exactly what a well-mannered young man would send.

From Warwick came a yellow rose nestled in a bed of red ones. The card read, "Beautiful and unique."

"Oh, did you get one from Warwick, too?" Athena shouted. "I did too—red roses and the note says, 'To a rare beauty.' " She leaned back in the pink chair that accented her fair beauty and her pale blond hair so well.

"It's obvious that you have snared another admirer." Aphrodite placed the roses back in their box and admired Mr. Horne's tribute. She sat across from her sister in a straightbacked chair, next to the carved table with lion's feet where she had placed her two bouquets. Her robe was of a dark green chambray, a color that complimented her light auburn hair and brought out the shades of green in her eyes. Not, of course, that she was in the least bit vain or cared to emphasize what others might consider her best points.

"Why would the man you say is my admirer send flowers to you?" Athena furrowed her perfect brow as she struggled to understand the concept.

"I would imagine he hopes to win me over so he will have success with you."

"Oh. How odd. Why would he do that, Ditie?"

"I would imagine he knows I do not approve of him and his crowd."

"But all of this is imagination?" Athena asked with rare insight. "I didn't think you were capable of such flights of fancy."

"It's not a flight of fancy, and it is more than my imagination. I do believe that is Warwick's plan."

Athena pondered this for a moment, her finger against the blush of her cheek. "I see. How flattering that Warwick would go to so much trouble. Should I reward him?"

"Athena, he is a . . ."

"Oh, Ditie, it is so easy to put you in a pelter. I was only funning."

Aphrodite did not find the remark amusing. Athena had spent the years since she began to develop into breathtaking young womanhood flirting with the most ineligible of men and boys. Aphrodite would never forget the first time she'd stumbled upon fourteen-year-old Athena being heartily kissed by the stable boy, an experienced youth of eighteen.

"Might I remind you that you have displayed an interest in the most unsuitable men."

"Oh, Ditie, don't be tiresome. You're not going to mention the time I was stranded in the rain with the squire's son."

"But the time with the soldier, Athena. Oh, that was nearly an unfortunate blot."

"It was only a kiss, Ditie. There's nothing wrong with a kiss."

"It's been more than one kiss, Athena. Every unacceptable . . ." Aphrodite began, then stopped herself. It would not, after all, do any good to be angry with Athena. The child enjoyed the company of males, any male, and kissing was a pleasant pastime for her. Nothing—no lectures, no frowns, no appeals to her virtue—had convinced the chit to behave properly. Even her parents agreed that the best solution was to marry her off quickly, while she still had her reputation. That was the reason she was spending a season in London when she was barely seventeen. It was up to Aphrodite to find for her sister a man she could admire and who would think her freshness appealing, a man of character who would not allow such antics.

"Oh, Ditie, I do try to be good, but sometimes I just can't help it." Athena clasped her hands in front of her, but Aphrodite knew she was far from being chastened. Athena's eyes and skin glowed. "Do you know how wonderful it is to kiss a man? To feel his lips soft against yours?"

That Aphrodite did, that a kiss had been bestowed upon her by Warwick two years earlier, was not a topic she would discuss with her younger sister or anyone else. Indeed, she had completely forgotten about it, she assured herself.

"Then," Athena continued, "then to have his lips become

hard and demanding? To have his hands moving across your back, pulling you closer and closer . . ."

"You need a husband, Athena, as soon as possible. I think perhaps Mr. Horne might be the right one." Aphrodite fanned herself with the young man's flowers until she noticed the petals were falling off with the force of her effort.

"Oh, Ditie, do you mind if I tell you I find him dull? He is nice looking, but he says things in such a solemn manner. Then, when I cannot understand what he said, he looks at me as if he thought I was stupid." Tears gathered in Athena's eyes.

"Now, now, darling, don't think that. You misunderstand him."

"Warwick, on the other hand." Athena stopped speaking and a look of pure delight crossed her perfect features. "What do you think his kisses would be like, Ditie?"

"I would prefer not to consider that."

"You would? I don't know how anyone could look at him and not wonder how it would feel to be in his arms, to have him look down at you with those wonderful blue eyes, to feel his muscular body pressed against yours."

"Athena, I believe we have discussed kisses enough for one day. Indeed, enough for a lifetime." Aphrodite placed her hand on her rapidly beating heart and attempted to slow it.

"Don't you ever wonder, Ditie? Don't you ever want to?"

"Of course not. Whatever you are about to say, it is not proper, Athena."

"But it must be normal, Ditie. Look at Mama and Papa."

"And look at the rest of society, Athena. Have you ever seen any married couple who behaves even remotely like our parents?"

"I wonder why they don't." Athena considered this for a moment. "Have you ever been kissed, Ditie?"

"Of course not," Aphrodite lied. "I am not the kind of woman men kiss, even if I thought it proper."

"I think you could be. You're very pretty. I've seen men look at you, but you glare at them. You frighten them."

"Then it would be a good idea for you to learn to do the same, little sister, if you expect to have a shred of reputation by the end of the season."

"I saw Warwick look at you last evening. I don't think he's interested in me if he looks at you in that way."

Aphrodite attempted to rein in her curiosity. She took another deep breath—goodness, she thought, Warwick was doing wonderful things for her lungs—then asked, "How . . . how was he looking at me?"

"With passion in his eyes."

"Oh, don't be absurd."

"Yes, Ditie, he was. When you weren't aware, he looked at your bosom. You have a lovely bosom. I've seen many men notice that."

"Well, they shouldn't." She straightened up, then realized such a position accentuated her form. Oh, she longed to ask more but was loath to encourage her imaginative sister. That's it, Aphrodite decided. It all came from Athena's whimsy. Warwick wasn't interested in her. Athena had fantasized it all. But, if he were . . .

Chapter Two

Oⁿ the following afternoon, Aphrodite approached the town house of her older sister, Terpsichore, with trepidation. Terpsi, named for the muse of music, dance, and lyric poetry, was known for her salons, to which she invited the literary lions and cubs of London.

Aphrodite hated the gatherings at Terpsi's small, elegant dwelling. In the first place, she thought her sister too young to have set up her own establishment, especially without a proper chaperone, but their parents had approved it, as they approved almost every foolhardy desire of their frivolous offspring.

But the main reason Aphrodite hated to attend was that the people were so strange. They discussed topics that she knew didn't belong in polite conversation. They discomfited her so much that Aphrodite invariably refused the invitations proffered to her each week. She wouldn't be going up the four steps and knocking on the scarlet door now if she didn't need to talk to her sister. Terpsi was the only other of her twelve siblings who was in town. In addition, Terpsi was possibly the only one with whom Aphrodite could share her disquietude and who might understand her worries about Athena.

The butler opened the door before Aphrodite could knock and ushered her into the parlors on the first floor. The rooms were so crowded that she couldn't find her sister. And dark—how could she possibly find anyone in the shadows? Here and there were candles, but the small pools of light did more to emphasize than illuminate the darkness.

"Dear, dear sister." Through the buzz of voices came a voice of round, clear tones from behind Aphrodite. "How delightful to see you."

When Aphrodite turned, she saw Terpsi was dressed in her usual odd way, with diaphanous scarves swirling from her waist, swirling around the floor and tied over her shoulder.

"Oh, my." Aphrodite gasped. "Your knees and—oh, my!—so much of your ... your ... you! can be seen through your skirt."

"Of course, dear sister. It's not a skirt." She twirled and displayed more flesh than Aphrodite believed a proper lady should exhibit, even to her husband. "It is only these lovely scarves."

Aphrodite lifted her eyes and inspected the chandelier, an activity she often engaged in when talking with her free-spirited sister. She sniffed. There was an aroma she couldn't describe, like burning flowers with a thick, heavy scent. "What's that smell?"

"Incense, dear sister. Isn't it lovely?" She led Aphrodite to an isolated corner. "Why are you here? You seldom deign to visit my salons."

"I need to discuss Athena with you."

"Ah, and has our little sister finally and inextricably blotted her copy book?" Terpsi led Aphrodite to a secluded corner.

"Not yet, but she is so impressionable." Aphrodite turned toward her sister, keeping her eyes on Terpsi's lovely face.

"You mean she'll kiss any personable young man. A stolen kiss is hardly death to her reputation, but you are worried." She tossed her braid of copper-colored hair over her shoulder as she arranged herself in a gilded chair and motioned Aphrodite to sit. "What can I do?"

"Perhaps if you were to talk to her. She believes *I* am irretrievably virtuous and lack a romantic spirit. She is correct, but I *do* know that if she continues snuggling with the servants she'll never receive a suitable offer."

"She is a good child at heart."

"Oh, as loving as she can be, but she needs to understand toward whom and in what situation it is appropriate. I know that in spite of your, well, your decidedly unusual ways and scandalous dress and odd mannerisms, you are a virtuous woman." Aphrodite paused and looked at her sister through narrowed eyes. "You *are* still a virtuous woman, are you not?"

"Of course, dear sister. I know only too well the fate of a woman of our class who is not married and is not chaste. I will certainly not surrender my virtue." Her eyes left Aphrodite's face and took on a seductive gleam. She licked her lower lip. "At least, not easily. Unless I find a very good reason to do so."

Aphrodite turned to follow the direction of Terpsi's eyes. "Oh, no, it is Warwick," she gasped and considered hiding under her chair. Terpsi stared at him like a tiger eyeing an appetizing jungle creature.

First he sent flowers to her, Aphrodite thought, then he flirted with Athena. Now Terpsi showed great—well, there was no other way to state it—lust for the man. The relationship was becoming incestuous.

"Yes," Terpsi breathed the word out. "Isn't he gorgeous? He'd be worth being compromised for, don't you think?"

Shocked, Aphrodite said, "Need I remind you of your responsibility to guard the family honor?"

"Oh, don't be such a cabbage-head, Ditie. Family honor is not nearly as enticing as Warwick."

"Then before you decide to compromise yourself, would you please talk to Athena? Remember, you are to discuss the importance of retaining her virginity. She'll listen to you. Perhaps." Aphrodite feared her face reflected her uncertainty about this last statement.

"Yes, dear, I will—but I will need to do it quickly, in case an opportunity with Warwick arises." Terpsi stood, looking beyond her sister. "Look, he's coming this way."

"I don't want to meet the man, Terpsi." Aphrodite turned her back and attempted to shrink in the spindly chair, her head down. She peeked from behind her shoulder as Terpsi held her hand out and Warwick grasped it.

"Warwick. How delightful to see you." Terpsi took his arm and attempted to stroll off with him, but the viscount refused to move.

"Isn't that your sister hiding in the corner?" He approached her and leaned down to look at her face. "Good afternoon, Lady Aphrodite. Are you attempting one of Lady Terpsichore's interesting exercises to strengthen your spine and improve your health?"

Aphrodite had no choice but to smile up at him and hold out her hand. "My lord. How delightful." She sat up and squared her shoulders. "I didn't realize you frequent my sister's salons."

"Of course. She has the most interesting literary talent here. Perhaps I could introduce you to some of them?"

"Oh, no, thank you. I was planning to leave. Please, continue to speak with your friends and associates." She lifted her eyebrows and blinked furiously at Terpsi, who stood behind Warwick, willing her sister to take the man with her.

"I would much prefer to stay with you. Do you, perhaps, have something in your eye?" He sat in the chair Terpsi had just vacated and pulled it closer to Aphrodite. "Let me see if I can help you." He placed one hand on her chin and tipped it up while he put his other on her forehead.

"What are you doing?" Aphrodite leaped to her feet. She looked around her, hoping no one had seen the man touching her. They were alone, which was unfortunate because she'd counted on Terpsi drawing Warwick off. "I'm fine."

"But your face . . . oh, I see. You were signaling your sister to take me with her. Lady Aphrodite, what have I ever done to you to make you wish to avoid me?"

"Oh, no, that's not it at all. This is for your sake. There is nothing about me, as a woman, that would interest you."

"Oh?" He lifted his brow. "Why would you say that? You are very attractive, in a sedate way."

"Now, my lord, that's coming a bit strong. I'm nothing like the rest of my family."

"I'm not so sure about that." He leaned toward her, his face only inches from hers, serious and intense.

She was aware of him: the scent of sandalwood, the touch of his breath against her cheek, his overwhelming masculinity.

He picked up her hand, turned it over, and placed his thumb on her palm, rubbing and caressing. "Your hands are lovely. Long fingers and soft skin." With his index finger, he traced her hand up her thumb, across her palm and fingers.

Drat the man, she thought. No one should be able to affect a woman like this. Her heart was beating tumultuously—surely he could hear it, she thought—and her breathing had almost stopped. She swallowed and took a deep breath before snatching her hand away from him. "Thank you, but it has been my experience that men don't look for pretty hands in a woman."

"Then they are fools. Of course, there is much more about you to admire than your graceful fingers." He looked in her eyes. "You are very beautiful. Your eyes sparkle and your cheeks are pink. Why do you suppose that is?"

"You know very well what it is," she snapped. "You cannot be unaware of your power over women. Now, if you would excuse me." She looked into his face. It was a mistake.

Usually, she was aware only of his extreme good looks, but under those thick brows, his eyes held a promise of pleasure unknown to her. She longed to touch the blue–black hair, to ruin the perfection of its arrangement, but with tremendous exertion of willpower, kept her hands in her lap. Quickly, she lowered her glance. Another unfortunate decision, because his broad shoulders were leaning toward her, and she wondered how it would feel to rest her head against them, to have the strength of his arms crushing her against his broad chest.

"Oh, my," Aphrodite gasped. "I do believe I should leave now."

But Warwick placed his hand on her shoulder. "Please, Lady Aphrodite, don't go yet. I wanted to ask you why you believe I would not find you captivating. Have I shown myself to be hard to please?"

"Of course not," she answered. "I come from a very attractive family, but I am aware that I am different. You know my sisters. Terpsichore is beautiful in a dramatic way; Athena is lovely, a sweet virgin." Aphrodite thought it was a good idea to remind Warwick of her sister's virtue.

"But Athena, for all her charm, is a child. You, Lady Aphrodite, are a woman."

"I am but twenty, my lord. Do you imply I'm on the shelf?"

"You know that's not what I'm saying. You are lovely, but I believe you could take more advantage of your charms. For example." He reached up and touched her hair. "You could allow curls around your face." He brushed his hand against her tightly woven hair style.

With a quick pat, she ascertained that her hair remained in its proper place. "I don't want to do that, my lord. That is not my style. Please, do not play with me."

"You are lovely." He studied her. "When you are angry, your eyes glow and you have such charming color. Perhaps you should be angry more often."

"I feel sure that, were I around you more often, I would be." She stood and attempted to walk around him, but he took her hands.

Aphrodite looked around her. Certainly someone, perhaps her dear sister, would see the hobble she was in and rescue her. Certainly this sort of thing wasn't normal behavior at a literary gathering, was it? But everyone was occupied in conversation. With the dim lighting, they might not even be able to see her. In another corner, someone was reading, and a group had gathered around him. Terpsi was nowhere to be seen.

"Perhaps if you were to modify the style of your clothing."

She could feel his eyes moving over her, assessing her dress and also her form. She had no reason to be ashamed of her frame. "I have not requested fashion advice," she said, then paused, curious, before allowing herself to ask, "What's the matter with my clothing? It is in the kick of fashion."

"Perhaps, among dowagers. My mother wears clothing more daring than yours."

Aphrodite stifled a remark about the seemliness of an older woman wearing low-cut gowns and said instead, "Perhaps I don't want to be as daring as your mother, or as anyone else. I am a virtuous woman."

"Ah, yes, you do flaunt your purity. Now, if you will

please sit down, let us talk about literature. I promise I will not tease you anymore if you will stop acting as if I am going to attack your virtue. Sometimes I forget you are not one of my usual flirts, but I promise to behave myself." He turned Aphrodite back toward her chair and seated her. "Have you read 'Childe Harold'? Tell me, what do you think of Byron?"

"I believe he's a fraud."

"Oh, and why is that?"

"He fools people. They have such an interest in his life, they will read anything he writes, even if most of it is overly romantic, dull, and poorly written."

"But even Lady Jersey likes Byron's poetry."

"Lady Jersey has never been my literary mentor."

"Well, I do agree with you, my lady. Then, may I ask your feelings toward Coleridge and Wordsworth?"

"Oh, much more to my taste. Are you familiar with 'Tintern Abbey'?"

They spent a few more minutes discussing poetry before Terpsi claimed Warwick and pulled him off to meet other people. Aphrodite stood, surprised at the depth Warwick had displayed, at least regarding poetry.

When Warwick disappeared into the darkness of the other parlors, Aphrodite felt a need to escape the town house. After making sure she had all her possessions, she hastened to the door, threw it open and hurried outside into the light of late afternoon. Once on the steps of the town house, Aphrodite tilted her face toward the sun and attempted to draw in every bit of warmth and brightness.

In the dimness, surrounded by the sweet scent of Terpsi's parlor, Warwick had woven a spell, Aphrodite decided as she allowed the brightness and warmth of the day to dissipate his magic. She had been almost intoxicated by the dimness and the seclusion and the soothing sound of his voice. *And the heat of his touch*, a little voice whispered. That was the lesson: she must *never* be alone with the man.

It was only a few days later that Aphrodite found herself in the park with Mr. Horne at the unfashionable hour of three o'clock.

"I have often thought it absurd to drive in the park at five just because that is the time society likes to be seen." Mr. Horne drove his modest cabriolet at a temperate speed through the nearly empty drives of Hyde Park.

"It is pleasant not to have to slow for the crowd," Aphrodite agreed. She looked down the leafy lanes and saw only a few people walking. "Of course, you don't see many people to greet at this time."

As they drove in silence, Aphrodite studied Mr. Horne, a slight young man with thinning brown hair combed in an unfashionably short style, but possessing a smile of great sweetness. His brown eyes squinted against the sun. She noted her escort's boots were buffed but not shiny and his coat was cut loosely. "I don't believe I have told you how much I appreciate your *habillement*. You are a gentleman who dresses for comfort."

"I have often thought those who stuff themselves into a constraining coat or pad their calves or wear high points that cut into their cheeks are foolish." His smile was gentle.

"I could not agree with you more. You are certainly not a dandy or a tulip of the *ton*," she complimented him. "You are a most commonplace young man."

"Thank you. My mother raised me to have no pretensions. My father was the younger son of a fine family but died when I was very young. My mother's father bought the lovely estate on which we now live. I will not have a title and will always be a gentleman farmer. I am happy with that."

"Do you have brothers or sisters?"

"No, I'm an only child."

How delightful to be an only child, Aphrodite thought, then banished the notion. She loved every one of her siblings, she reminded herself.

"Tell me about your family, Lady Aphrodite."

A sure way to frighten him, she thought. "You have met my parents."

"Oh, yes, the romantic Marquis and Marchioness of Temple. Who doesn't know them?"

"And you've met my younger sister, Athena."

"A lovely young woman."

"Perhaps you've met my older sister Terpsichore? She holds a famous literary salon."

"I do not know much about literature, my lady. I hope that doesn't disturb you. My mother always believed it was frivolous, if you will forgive me for saying that. I was brought up reading sermons and have never felt the need for lighter, less improving material."

"Certainly, Mr. Horne. As to the rest of my family, I have ten other brothers and sisters."

"Oh, yes, I'd heard your mother was . . ."

She knew he wanted to say that he'd heard of her mother's fecundity but she refused to supply the word.

"I mean, my, what a large family," he substituted. "You must enjoy your holidays together. I must admit, when I heard about such a large family, I realized how much I miss having at least one sibling. But I am blessed to have my beloved mother. Please tell me more."

"Do you know my brother Aeolus?"

"Yes, he was at Cambridge with me. What is he doing now?" Mr. Horne turned the carriage down another deserted path.

"He's in Africa, searching for the source of the Nile."

"How interesting. Has he started in Egypt?"

"No, he has a theory that the source of the Nile is close

to the source of the Congo, so he is traveling east on that river."

"Oh?" Mr. Horne blinked and looked at Aphrodite. "On what does he base his theory? Are there some historical writings that suggest this?"

"He bases this on his own opinion. Mr. Horne, you must realize that a Herrington doesn't have to have a reason to believe what he or she believes. They just . . . believe."

"Isn't there great danger in Africa now?"

"Mr. Horne, danger is the *raison d'être* to a Herrington. Aeolus loves risk."

"And your father? Your father actually allowed his heir to dash off to Africa?"

"My father is, of course, a Herrington. He understands Aeolus's craving for danger. When he was barely sixteen, my father attempted to go to the colonies to fight for the king. He was disconsolate because the war ended before he was able to smuggle himself out of the country. His father, the Fourth Marquis of Temple, thought it a marvelous lark."

"Oh." He glanced sideways at her.

"I am not like the other Herringtons, Mr. Horne," she reassured him with a smile. "I love them dearly but we are different."

"I believe I met your sister Artemis, before she married Sanderson. Please excuse me for asking this. I know little of what happens in London because I spend so little time in society. I enjoy most taking care of our estate and chatting with my mother. Where is your sister now?"

"She and her husband are exploring the wilderness on the frontier of the colonies. In a dreadful wasteland called Kentucky. I believe that's how the place is pronounced."

The cabriolet lurched as Mr. Horne pulled back on the reins. "She's in the colonies? Exploring the wilderness. But the danger! How could her husband allow her to do this?"

"Once Artemis makes up her mind, no one can change it. However, it was her husband's idea. They are well matched."

Mr. Horne gulped. "You say they are in Ken-tucky? Where is that?"

"It used to be part of Virginia."

"Oh, yes, I've heard of that colony." He snapped the reins and the horses quickened their gait. "And the rest of your family?"

"My brother Asklepios is at Cambridge. As you might guess from his name, he is very interested in medicine but, other than showing high spirits, he has done nothing too unusual. At home, I have four younger brothers and three sisters."

"My, my." Mr. Horne didn't speak for a few moments, so deep was he in thought. After that long pause, he brought up a few subjects but the conversation languished as the topics of agreement ran out, and there was no one in the park to discuss.

As he stopped the carriage in front of the Herrington town house, Mr. Horne continued his thoughtful attitude as he helped Aphrodite descend. "I wonder," he said as he escorted her up the steps, "if I could call on your father in the morning? I have something I would like to discuss with him."

"I am certain he would be delighted to speak with you. My father prides himself on his use of modern farming methods. Perhaps you have heard of his interest? I believe you have a great deal in common."

Mr. Horne's fair skin flushed and he tugged at the neck of his shirt. "No, Lady Aphrodite, it is something of a personal nature I wish to discuss with him, and then with you." He bowed and turned toward his vehicle. "If you will excuse me. I will plan to see your father at noon, if that will be convenient."

"I feel sure it will be." Aphrodite nodded at him but felt a little dazed. She was going to receive an offer from this pleasant man.

He would make a fine husband, she thought. They would be comfortable. Never would she feel blood pounding through her body with Mr. Horne. Never would he befuddle her brain or interrupt her breathing. She attempted to convince herself that she felt relief, but a nagging doubt whispered that she would miss the tumult Warwick could evoke with a glance.

Chapter Three

"**O**h, my darling Aphrodite, I am so proud of you." Hazel, the Marchioness of Temple, took her daughter by the hands and twirled her around the room. Her blond curls swirled across a lovely, flushed face, and her robe of willow green muslin twirled around her slim figure. "So very, very proud."

Her mother's excitement confused Aphrodite. After she'd removed her pelisse and entered her mother's parlor to ask when her father would be home, Mama had run toward her with a smile and started dancing. Certainly she couldn't have heard about Mr. Horne's offer yet. "Why are you proud of me, Mama?" she asked.

"Never would I have thought it of you, dearest. Terpsichore, yes, and Athena when she's a little older— although she is not much of a challenge. But for this to happen to my prim daughter! Well, I never would have believed it." The Marchioness stopped twirling and tumbled onto an elegant Egyptian couch.

A little dizzy, Aphrodite asked, "How did you hear of this so quickly?"

"Your father told me. It happened just this morning, and, dear man, he stopped by on his way to Tattersall's to tell me."

"Do you mean that Mr. Horne has already spoken to him?"

"No, dear, not Mr. Horne. Warwick."

"Warwick wants to marry me? How odd." Aphrodite tilted her head as she considered this. She experienced a strange but pleasant reaction and smiled.

"Not marriage, dearest. The wager."

"Mama, please tell me what has happened." Aphrodite settled herself against the curved arm of the sofa to listen.

"The betting book at White's. *You* are in the betting book." The Marchioness clapped her hands together.

"I am?" Aphrodite sat up so quickly she almost fell off the sofa. "Whatever for?"

"Warwick has wagered five hundred guineas—five hundred guineas, my dear!—that he will be able to melt the ice and kiss you."

Aphrodite collapsed back. "How insulting."

"Oh, dearest, I was afraid you'd think that, but it's not, you know. In certain circles, to be in the betting book is an achievement." She lowered her impossibly long lashes. "When I first came out, there were no fewer than seven wagers about me. Only your father won, of course."

It was useless to attempt to explain her feelings, Aphrodite knew. "How interesting," she said. "I'm glad I made you proud."

"Oh, dear, you aren't happy about this." The Marchioness placed her hand on her daughter's. "Why is that, darling?"

"It's just that we're so very different, Mama. The things that interest you and are important to you aren't to me. I mean, everyone else in this family follows their impulses.

They don't care what other people think. I find that very uncomfortable."

"I'm sorry, dear. Even as bubbleheaded as I am, I know that there are times you feel unlike the rest of us. That's why I found this wager so exciting. It is something we have in common."

"Oh, Mama. I have nothing in common with anyone else in this family."

"Of course you do, dear Ditie."

"What is one thing I have in common with you and Papa and Terpsi and Athena, except blood?"

The Marchioness wrinkled her lovely brow but said nothing.

"We have nothing in common," Aphrodite said. "Except we all have terrible names."

The Marchioness gasped. "They are lovely names! My darling, I worked so hard to find you a name to fit you exactly. When you were a baby, you loved to be held and kissed. That's why we named you for Aphrodite, the goddess of love."

"I'd rather have been Susan or Augusta or anything but Aphrodite."

"I gave you such beautiful names because my own is so plain—Hazel."

"What's wrong with that, Mama? Everyone can spell it and pronounce it."

"What's the matter with a name like Hazel?" She looked at her daughter, tears gathering in her luminous eyes. "Look how beautiful I am—and I was named after a nut."

"Oh, Mama, please forgive me. I've made you sad." Aphrodite reached for a handkerchief. "I'm just feeling out of sorts today. I love my name. Thank you. And you are the most magnificent Hazel in the world."

The Marchioness blew her nose, daintily. "It's hard to feel beautiful when your name is Hazel."

"And I don't mind about the wager," Aphrodite lied. "I'm glad you're excited about it."

"Oh, I'm delighted, my dear." Her mother wiped her eyes then patted Aphrodite's hand. "What is this you were saying about Mr. Horne?"

"He wants to see father tomorrow at noon."

"An offer. How wonderful. An offer from Mr. Horne. He's a most sincere young man. How do you feel about his offer?"

Aphrodite could not put her emotions into words. Hearing about the wager by Warwick reinforced her earlier decision. It would be better to be married and safe from him. Was it cowardly to use Mr. Horne this way? No, she thought. She'd be a loyal and loving wife. It would be a good marriage. Not as passionate as her parents', but that could be counted as an advantage.

In addition, it was the only offer she had received. She had no desire to be a maiden aunt to what was certain to be an enormous brood of nephews and nieces. The sober young men who interested her were always scared away by her family, and the men that flirted with her *because* of her family she found to be shallow and foolish.

"I'm very pleased," she said.

"Then your father and I will be happy with you." Her mother enfolded Aphrodite in a hug, patting her back. "Oh, my dear, we'll plan the most amazing wedding."

Aphrodite shuddered.

After Mr. Horne's arrival the next morning, Aphrodite waited in the parlor with her mother while he spoke with her father. It was nearly twelve-thirty when the Marquis ushered the young man into the room.

"I believe Mr. Horne would like to speak to Aphrodite in private," he said to his wife.

"Of course, my love." The Marchioness rose, kissed her

daughter on the cheek, and left the room on her husband's arm.

Neither Mr. Horne or Aphrodite spoke for a minute. He walked across the wide expanse of gold carpet, sat in a chair opposite her instead of the sofa next to his future betrothed, and cleared his throat. "I have spoken to your father and believe we have reached an understanding."

"Yes?"

"I would like you to marry me."

"How nice," Aphrodite murmured. "I would be very happy to marry you."

He smiled. "I, too, am delighted. However, before we announce our engagement, I would like you to visit our estate, Windwillow, to meet my mother. I am sure she will be delighted with you and you with her, but before we make our engagement public, I would like her approval."

"Of course." Why did she feel relief that the engagement was not to be revealed immediately?

"I must tell you this. My mother has heard of your family."

"Yes?" Aphrodite drew herself up and fixed him with a piercing gaze.

"As you know, they are somewhat, well, infamous." His cheeks flushed under her stare.

"I beg your pardon?" Aphrodite glared at him. Her family might drive her wild, but she allowed no one else to criticize them. "You are speaking of my family."

"I apologize. That was a poor choice of words. I have found you to be conscientious and responsible, but my mother needs to meet you and learn that for herself."

"In other words, your mother wants to know if I am different from the rest of my family before I am allowed to join hers?" Her betrothed hardly seemed transported by love but then, neither was she, Aphrodite thought.

"I wouldn't state it quite so bluntly. We live quietly. I

don't know if someone like, oh, like your sister, Lady Athena, would be happy in the country. In addition, you and I have not been acquainted for long. We do want to make sure that we are suited, do we not?" He stood and bowed over her, taking her hand.

Mollified, she said, "Of course. That sounds sensible."

"And so, I am arranging a small house party for next month and hope that you and your parents and any other members of your family will be able to stay with us for a fortnight. The guests will include only family and a few close friends. In that way, you can get to know my mother, an exceptional woman, as I've said. I know you will admire her."

"I'm sure I will."

"And there is, of course, something about your family that my mother is sure to admire."

"What is that?" She wrinkled her brow, trying to guess what about her family could possibly impress the admirable Mrs. Horne.

"Your mother's remarkable fruitfulness."

"I beg your pardon." With a leap, she came to her feet.

"Oh, I know such a conversation would not be proper in society but we are, after all, almost betrothed, and I feel I must discuss this with you."

"One of the reasons you want to marry me is because I have so many brothers and sisters?" She stared at him.

"It was one of the things that first attracted me to you. I told you that I'm an only child. It is my mother's dearest wish to dandle a quiver of grandchildren on her knee. She will make the most excellent of grandmothers."

"You want to marry me so I can give your mother grandchildren?" Aphrodite spun and walked to the window. She looked out at the traffic on the street.

"There are other reasons. I believe you and I share the same interests, that we will live quiet and comfortable lives together." She could hear his voice coming closer to her. "Of course, I must choose a woman my mother will accept. The extreme fertility of your family is just an added incentive." He paused. "Have you made your decision too precipitously? Would you like more time to consider?"

It wasn't unusual, Aphrodite reflected. Certainly a man wanted an heir, or in Mr. Horne's case, many heirs. A wife's duty was to present him with such tributes. For a moment, she pictured herself surrounded by twelve children: some tugging on her skirt, others sobbing in her arms, still others jumping and running from her. She almost fled, but she knew the scene she envisioned was unrealistic. There would be an army of nursery maids and governesses.

But she would still have to give birth to all of them. And conceive them with this man whom, as he said, she hardly knew.

On the other hand, there was the dangerous lure of Warwick, who had no intention of marriage. In truth, she had no other prospects.

She turned and looked up at him. "Yes, I'll be happy to spend a fortnight at your estate. I shall discuss this with my parents."

"You have made me the happiest of men." He leaned down to kiss her cheek.

"And I," Aphrodite whispered the words through lips she forced to smile. "I am the happiest of women."

"Mama? Papa?" Aphrodite knocked on the door of her parents' chambers and waited. "It is I, Aphrodite."

"Come in, darling," her mother shouted.

The apartment consisted of a parlor with an adjoining bedroom. The walls were blue and white striped, the carpet was blue and the furniture was blue, and white. It was the perfect background for a blond, as were all the rooms in the townhouse.

As she had feared, the Marquis was sitting in a comfortable blue chair and her mother was snuggled in his arms. *When does desire begin to fade?* she wondered.

"Mama, Papa, Mr. Horne has asked me to visit his family at their country estate for a fortnight in a few weeks. He hopes that you will be able to accept the invitation of his esteemed mother."

"Oh, dear." The Marchioness slid from her husband's lap. "I was just imparting a tidbit of interesting news to your father."

"Oh, Mama, no! Not again."

"Yes, darling. You will soon have another darling brother or sister."

"Mama! Papa! Again?"

The Marquis stood. "Am I not the most fortunate of men? To have married a woman of such perfection and fecundity?"

It wouldn't do any good to remonstrate with them. Aphrodite had attempted to explain how embarrassing such productivity was six years earlier, when Ceto was born—then Demeter and Hepaestus appeared—and now this poor infant, who would assume another unpronounceable, unspellable Greek name.

"Papa, you are truly blessed." Aphrodite kissed her mother's cheek.

"But because of my interesting condition, we will not be able to visit your young man's estate. Your Papa insists that we go home now, so I can rest on the estate." She settled herself on a chair and patted the seat of the one next to her, inviting Aphrodite to join her. "You know how he hates for me to travel during this time, but I will write a nice letter of explanation."

"Oh, no. I'll tell Mr. Horne and he can relay that to his mother." Aphrodite was not prepared to have the *ton* know so soon that the fourteenth Herrington was on the way.

"It seems a havey-cavey way to handle this," the Marchioness began.

"Oh, no. Mr. Horne says this will be a very informal house party."

The Marquis reached across the distance that separated them and patted his daughter's knee. "We shall invite them to the estate, perhaps for a family Christmas."

"You will need to take a chaperone. Terpsi will go with you, to lend countenance," the Marchioness said.

"Mama, Terpsi will hardly add countenance. It would be better for me to go alone. This is just a family gathering."

The Marchioness' eyes widened. "Oh, my dear, that will never do. I have heard, although I've never met her, I have heard that Mrs. Horne is a very proper woman. You will need a chaperone."

"I will have Mignon," Aphrodite insisted. Surely her mother knew that the house party would be much calmer and far easier for her without her high-spirited older sister.

Her mother groaned. "My dear, you know better. Mignon is your dresser."

"Mama, Terpsi is . . . eccentric," Aphrodite pleaded.

"Unusual, perhaps," her father agreed. "But she is still a lady of standing."

"Yes, Papa." Aphrodite bowed her head and accepted the inevitable.

"And you will need to take Athena with you," Mama added.

"Oh, Mama, no! Why?" Her eyes lifted as she spun to stare at her mother. "You know how fastidious she is. She does *not* like the country. She says she gets the hem of her dress dirty in the grass and is always stepping in something."

"Dear Athena will not want to leave London and return home with us during the season. With you gone, there is no one in town I would trust to watch over her." The Marchioness stared at Aphrodite. "You know what I mean by that."

"Yes, Mama," she agreed with a sigh. Now, not only would she have to try to become better acquainted with her betrothed, meet and impress Mrs. Horne, but she would have to make sure that Terpsi didn't do anything outrageous and that Athena didn't find too many young footmen who looked handsome in their livery.

"It is so wonderful to have a levelheaded daughter we can trust to take care of everything." The Marchioness patted Aphrodite's hand.

All things considered, Aphrodite was getting tired of these little pats. Each one meant she was taking on another onerous responsibility.

"And you can plan your wedding for about nine months from now," the Marquis promised.

Among the Herringtons, time was measured differently, Aphrodite reflected. In her family, a year was calculated on a calendar of nine months in length.

Chapter Four

Mrs. Horne looked like a toad, Aphrodite thought. An enormous white toad, lurking on a huge green lily pad. Her beady little eyes glittered, bright and malevolent. They followed Aphrodite's every step across the room as if, any second, a long tongue would dart out from this creature and snatch her.

"Come here, girl." When Mrs. Horne spoke, her mouth barely moved and no tongue issued from it, but with each word she rapped on the floor with a thick wooden cane.

And to think she had hurried to meet this woman.

Aphrodite had arrived at Windwillow only minutes earlier. When Frederick's well-sprung town coach stopped in front of the mansion, she was enthralled by its beauty. Soft pink brick with white trim reached far to the left and right.

"How lovely." Aphrodite slowly descended from the carriage and turned to admired the lush green park in front of the house. "I want to see it all."

"Later, Aphrodite, later. My mother wants to meet you immediately." Mr. Horne took her elbow and hurried her up the graceful front steps and through the door held by an impassive butler. "I've told Mother how much she'll like you. You have a rare surprise ahead in meeting her."

While her shoes tapped across the marble floor of the enormous entrance hall, Aphrodite turned to study the magnificence of the hexagonal hall. A life-sized statue of a Greek god, tastefully draped, stood in each angle. The ceiling soared three stories, held up by six magnificent columns, and a curving staircase arose from the middle of the entranceway and floated to the top story. An imposing fireplace graced one side of the hall. Enormous paintings hung on the other walls. Aphrodite would have loved to examine the entire area, but when she reached out to rub her fingers across the cool grain of one of the marble columns, Mr. Horne took her arm and hurried her toward the wide staircase.

"This is Morgan." He gestured toward a young woman in a plain brown gown with a stiff white apron. "She'll take you to your chambers now and help you refresh yourself. My mother will expect you in her parlor in ten minutes."

"Ten minutes," Aphrodite gasped. "I don't think I can be ready so quickly."

"If you don't hurry, Mother will be so disappointed. The darling can be so impatient when she has a treat coming. She doesn't like to wait."

Although the trip in Mr. Horne's comfortable carriage had lasted for only five hours, Aphrodite still wished for an hour to wash off the dirt of the journey, change clothes, and rest. She barely had time to reach the suite, remove her hat, and wash her hands before Morgan mentioned, hesitantly, that Mrs. Horne had requested her *immediate* presence in the parlor.

Aphrodite studied herself in the mirror. Hair straggled down her neck and there was a smudge on her left cheek. What was it? she wondered as she splashed water on the dirt. Aphrodite looked down at her traveling gown, which was wrinkled and dusty. She needed to change, but Mignon had yet to arrive with the luggage. "Please tell Mrs. Horne I will be down as soon as Mignon arrives. I must change my clothes and have her arrange my hair."

The maid paled slightly. "I beg your pardon, my lady, but *no one* refuses to do what Mrs. Horne asks." She curtsied. "If you would please come with me?"

Aphrodite rubbed at the smudge on her face and patted her hair in place with her hands, then turned to follow Morgan to meet the wonderful woman who was to be her mother-in-law. There was a flutter of nerves in her stomach as well as a feeling of joyful anticipation. She faced a new beginning, an important change in her life.

Frederick's mother truly looked like a toad. She was enormously fat but not jolly. The behemoth was dressed in white with ruffles and flounces and furbelows that magnified her bulk. Her face looked like an overstuffed pillow with nasty, glittering eyes, a lump of a nose, and a straight line of lips that looked as if they never smiled. As Aphrodite moved farther into the room, she was aware of a musty smell, like unwashed clothing and stale food.

But, Aphrodite thought, Frederick loves her. She is probably a lovely woman. Inside.

"Looks too skinny to breed," Mrs. Horne barked, then turned to her son. "Much too skinny. No hips."

Aphrodite swirled to look at Horne, expecting him to protect her from his mother's vicious words, but he nodded his head in agreement.

"That's what I thought at first, Mother." He approached his mother's throne and leaned down to kiss the cheek she held up for him. "But her stock is impeccable. She has twelve brothers and sisters, and her mother is still young."

"Ah, I know all about those Herringtons, but she . . ." Mrs. Horne pointed toward Aphrodite with her cane. "She don't look big enough to have a brood."

"I assure you that the Marchioness is very slender and yet bears children with great ease."

"Come here, girl!" Mrs. Horne shook her cane at Aphrodite.

Aphrodite looked behind her. Surely the woman spoke to a servant, not to her. But there was no one else in the room. "Do you mean me?" She took a few steps toward Mrs. Horne, who was ensconced in an enormous muddy green chair.

"Turn around, girl." The grimy shawls that protected the woman from a draught Aphrodite couldn't feel shook as Mrs. Horne pounded the cane on the floor again.

Aphrodite blinked. "Frederick?" He nodded at her.

"Go on, girl. Turn around!" the toad shouted again.

Instead, Aphrodite walked forward and held out her hand. "I am Aphrodite Herrington. So pleased to meet you. Your son has spoken of you with such great affection."

"Of course he has. He's a good boy. Knows his duty." Mrs. Horne thumped on the floor with her cane. "Turn around, girl. Let me see you."

Aphrodite looked at the floor, where the cane had worn a hole in the dark brown carpet. "How delighted I am to be here. What a lovely home you have." She gave Mrs. Horne her most winning smile.

"Are you deaf, girl? I said turn around." Mrs. Horne's enormous bosom quivered with the pounding of her cane.

Instead, Aphrodite said, "May I?" She sat in a chair next to the woman and fanned herself with her hand. The room was stifling, especially so close to the blazing fireplace. "Please tell me about the other guests you are expecting."

"What's the matter with the chit?" Mrs. Horne shouted at her son.

"Nothing, Mother. I believe you just need to get to know each other."

"Well, then, girl, tell me about your family."

"My parents . . ."

"No, no." She banged on the floor with the cane again. "Tell me about your brothers and sisters. Twelve? How old are they?"

"My oldest brother is Aeolus. He's in Africa . . ."

"I don't care what he's doing."

"He is twenty-five."

"Girl, what I want to know is, does he have any children?"

"He is not married." Aphrodite waited for a moment for another question but the woman just pounded on the floor again. "My sister Artemis is twenty-four," Aphrodite continued. "She's married but has no children."

"Why not?" Mrs. Horne demanded.

"We have not discussed it," Aphrodite said in an icy voice. Did the woman have no understanding of manners or privacy? Aphrodite vowed to discuss this with her fiancé. "Next is Terpsichore, twenty-two. She will be here shortly, with my sister Athena in our father's travelling carriage."

"Humph," Mrs. Horne grumbled. "I've heard about her. Fast. Wears odd clothes. Go on." She waved her cane at Aphrodite.

"I am next, then my brother Asklepios is eighteen; Athena is seventeen. She's coming with Terpsichore. At home are the twins, Ares and Celina who are fourteen." Aphrodite ticked them off on her fingers. "Ceto, twelve; Helios, ten; Eurus, seven; Demeter, four; and Hepaestus is an infant."

Mrs. Horne leaned back in her chair with a sigh of satisfaction and, Aphrodite was amazed to note, a smile. "You have chosen well, son."

"Thank you, Mama."

"But terrible names." She leaned forward and wagged her finger at Aphrodite. "You name your children good

English names: Samuel and Eleanor and Frederick and Matilda."

Aphrodite bristled. "I think we all have lovely names. My parents chose them with love and great care. They wanted the perfect name for each of us."

"They made a lot of mistakes, didn't they, girl?" She emitted a dry, choking sound that Aphrodite guessed was a laugh.

Aphrodite cringed.

"Leave, girl. Go on. Get out." The stick *thunked* against the floor again. "Go to your chambers. I want to talk with my son."

Aphrodite glanced up at Frederick who remained at his mother's side. With a nod and smile at Aphrodite, he said, "I'll see you at dinner." Then he picked up his mother's hand. "I haven't seen Mother for weeks and I need to catch up with the old dear's gossip."

The old dear, indeed! *What a nasty old woman,* Aphrodite thought as she swirled to get out of the fetid atmosphere. She threw the door open, dashed into the hall, and took a deep breath of the cool, sweet-smelling air.

As she slowly recovered from the horrific experience of meeting Mrs. Horne, she noticed Warwick lounging against the wall across from the parlor.

Her mouth dropped. "What are you doing here?" she demanded. Then, embarrassed at her rudeness and the fact that he'd seen her when she was obviously upset, she almost went back into the parlor and locked the door. Only the thought of the gargoyle on the other side kept her in place.

She's been through a terrible ordeal, Warwick thought. Her lovely skin was mottled, probably from the heat and strain, the lovely reddish-blond hair was disordered, and light violet blotches colored the fair skin under her eyes. Exhaustion and shock, he thought. She'd drooped until she saw him. Then the look on her face showed that he was the last person she expected—or wanted—to see.

As Warwick pushed himself away from the wall, he said, "So you have met my dear aunt?"

"Oh? I didn't realize you were related to the Horne family." She attempted a pleasant conversational tone.

"It is not a connection I mention often. When my father's youngest brother married the fair and very wealthy Matilda Horne, he had to assume that name to share the fortune. My father is the head of the family and asked me to represent him at this gathering, to welcome you into our family."

"Oh." She seemed to sort through responses until she finally said, "How delightful."

It was obvious she was shaken, as would be any young woman who'd just met such a Gorgon and realized what her life would be like with Matilda Horne as her *belle-mère*, but she tried not to show it. He admired that. Pluck to the backbone.

The gossip that Frederick was bringing home a young woman for his mother's inspection had titillated the family. If Warwick hadn't known Aphrodite, he probably would have left the young woman to her fate, but he had accepted the invitation because he guessed Aphrodite had no idea of what awaited her.

What a shock to walk into the lair of Matilda Horne.

Why did he care?

He did not owe Aphrodite anything. Why had he hastened to Windwillow? Certainly not to rescue her. Well, perhaps that was part of the reason. He felt sorry for her. Horne was a good enough chap, but Frederick would never guard his wife from the woman he called his beloved mother. Aphrodite had a spark of spirit. The thought of it being crushed by that monster bothered him. It must be, he

decided, his sense of justice. It was only fair that someone
help her make a decision about her future.

But why did *he* care? He never bothered himself with
other people, but he could not force back the thought that
if Frederick had brought any other young woman home as
his prospective bride, he would not have cared a whit.

He found Aphrodite interesting and attractive. A few
years ago, he'd courted her for a sennight, a day or two
longer than he usually courted a young woman. Although
it had been a pleasant interlude, he had not been tempted
to make an offer. When he married, it would not be for
love. He didn't believe in love. He'd marry when it was
time for him to do his duty for his family.

He'd enjoyed flirting with her, and still did. He believed
that she'd been more attracted to him than he was to her,
those few years ago. Even after she'd cut him cold for no
reason he could imagine, he couldn't forget a light, sweet
kiss he'd stolen long ago, even though he'd kissed many
women much more experienced than she.

That one kiss? Was that why was he putting himself out
for her? Certainly not.

She deserved a better life than that found in Matilda
Horne's home. He'd do his good deed, chat with her to
make her feel better, maybe even steal another kiss or two
as he tried to steer her away from Frederick and the ordeal
of living with Matilda Horne. Then he'd be on his way.

His actions weren't all unselfish, he knew. There was an
imp that lived within him. His sister said he found amusement in the most peculiar places and in the oddest situa-
tions.

The imp had come forth when he'd heard that Terpsi and
Athena accompanied their sister. The addition of those tem-
pestuous personalities and the efforts of Aphrodite to control them held all the elements of a farce. He'd been bored,

and the fortnight should prove amusing. Perhaps he could stir up the brew at the same time he did a good deed.

But he still didn't know why he cared, didn't have the slightest idea why he should put himself out for Aphrodite Herrington. His decision had been based on more than the odd propensity for entertainment or that imp within him. As soon as he'd heard of the gathering, he had almost bullied his father into sending him to represent the family without a thought or pause, except to tell his valet Taylor to pack and follow him in the whiskey. Then he'd leaped on his horse and ridden hard for Windwillow.

Why? He wasn't sure he wanted to identify the reason and so he moved his thoughts past it.

Immediately upon his arrival, his sister told him that Aphrodite had been summoned to see that terrible woman. With a speed that would have caused his valet to threaten to leave, Warwick brushed and straightened his own clothing, attempted to arrange his hair into something close to the style that Taylor turned him out in, and arrived to await Aphrodite outside the parlor door only seconds before she emerged, looking as if she'd faced Lucifer himself and barely survived. But she had survived. He admired her.

Warwick offered his arm. "If I may take you for a walk? It will soothe your nerves."

"I can't." Aphrodite caught sight of herself in the mirror. "My hair." She attempted to shove the strands back in place. "And my dress." She brushed at the worst of the wrinkles. "Oh, and my face." She stared at herself in the mirror, obviously aware that the damage done by the trip and the subsequent meeting with Mrs. Horne could not be repaired in a trice. "But thank you," she said as she remembered her manners. "You are very kind."

"I'm not a bit kind, as you well know. I've just arrived and would like to take a walk. You need some fresh air and a few minutes to recover from your interview."

She glanced up at him, her brow furrowed as Warwick continued.

"Horne has a lovely estate. You should see it, to help you decide if the beauty of this site will make up for spending the rest of your life with his mother." He offered his arm again, and this time she took it.

He guided her out the door and down the steps toward a path that wound down to the lake. Large trees on each side shaded the trail but enough light filtered through to make lacy shadows on the stones.

After they strolled for a few minutes, Aphrodite sighed. "This is lovely. And very peaceful."

"Would you like to rest on this bench? There's a lovely view of the lake."

She sat and studied the brilliant blue of the lake and the glistening white of the ruins on the island. They could hear voices and laughter.

"Don't they sound happy?" Aphrodite smiled up at him.

She lacked Terpsi's flash and Lady Athena's ethereal beauty, he reflected, but how very naturally lovely she was. Her light auburn hair reflected the filtered sunlight, which also added a glow to her skin. A neat figure, too, he thought. If she could unbend just a little, be a bit more of a Herrington, they could have a delightful flirtation as the drama unfolded. Did he care that she was almost betrothed to Frederick? Not at all. After all, he wasn't willing to take his cousin's place in the parson's mousetrap, but a flirtation might save her from making a terrible mistake. He would sacrifice himself with the most altruistic of motives.

"Oh, my, it is beautiful." She studied the view of the vast estate while Warwick sat on the marble railing surrounding the bench. "I had no idea Windwillow was such a lovely place. Frederick doesn't act like a wealthy man."

"No, Frederick is a very pleasant young man. The money comes from his mother, my dear Aunt Matilda. She is the daughter of a rich merchant who brought a much-needed infusion of wealth to my father's youngest brother Bernard. At the time, it seemed advantageous. However, it is said Uncle Bernard died with a smile on his face because he was escaping his dear wife."

"Oh." She considered that for a moment. "Marrying a wealthy woman to replenish the family coffers is hardly unusual."

"Not at all," Warwick agreed.

After they had both studied the vista in silence for a few minutes, he continued. "I believe you need to know that Aunt Matilda has always stated that the sorrow of her life is that she was blessed with only one child. That's why she has always insisted that Frederick's bride be a good breeder."

Aphrodite jumped to her feet. "My goodness!"

"I apologize if you feel my comment was indelicate," Warwick said. "I thought you should know that the entire family knows of your—how should I say this?— endowment. Perhaps gift might be a better word."

"Oh, dear." She covered her cheeks with her hands. "I shall never be able to face them."

"I considered not telling you this, but Aunt Matilda is likely to bellow the information out at any time. I thought you should be warned."

"Oh, yes. Thank you." She dropped back on the bench. "Frederick had told me, and she was so interested in my family, but I didn't realize that everyone knows that my parents . . . oh, dear." A lovely pink colored her cheeks. "They all know that my large family is what recommended me to Frederick?"

"I'm sure there is more to his choice than that. You are very lovely and, after all, there must be three or four other young women on the marriage mart who come from large families."

She turned disheartened eyes toward him. "Not as large as mine."

"No, but as I remember, Lady Sophia Jeffrey has seven siblings. And Miss Pemberton has six. After a certain number, I believe they are all equal."

"Sophia has a twitch, and Miss Pemberton has that terrible laugh." She covered her mouth and looked up at him quickly. "Oh, please forgive me. I never discuss the faults of others."

"Such statements are clearly an indication of your agitation." He sat on the bench and took her hand. "I'm sure it was your many charms that attracted Frederick." When she didn't reply, Warwick continued. "And you'll have many years together—you and Frederick and Mrs. Horne." He chuckled to himself as her mouth dropped open.

"Many years together?" She clutched at his hand.

"Oh, Aunt Matilda is quite young. Frederick was born when she was seventeen. He's twenty-four now. She's forty-one."

"Only forty-one?"

"Oh, yes, the three of you will have twenty, thirty, perhaps even forty or more years together. Unless Frederick were to die first. Then it would be you and dear Matilda together, until one of you dies."

"Thirty or forty more years?" She looked up at him, her eyes distressed. "Oh, dear. Do you really think she'll live that long?"

"Oh, undoubtedly. She comes from a healthy family. Her great uncle is Josiah Horne."

She gasped. "You mean the man they call Methuselah?"

"Yes." He nodded and patted her hand. "One-hundred-and-four on his last birthday and still in good health. They say time has not softened his tongue. As vicious as ever. Just think, Aunt Matilda might live for sixty or more years."

"I would be eighty." Aphrodite swallowed hard.

"That's true. Sixty years with Matilda Horne."

He could tell that she was considering the next sixty years with dread. Her shoulders drooped. Then she sat up.

"But she'll be in the dower house. Certainly she wouldn't live with Frederick and me."

"Frederick is a good son. He'd never throw his mother from her home. Besides, she wants to be around to spoil those dozens of children you're going to have." With every sentence, he watched her head fall and her shoulders curve inward.

"He tells me she is wonderful, admirable," she whispered.

"He has always been a most dutiful son."

"But we didn't get along very well, Mrs. Horne and I."

"She has a strong personality."

"Yes." Aphrodite stood and took a deep breath. "This view is lovely. I would like to see the lake. Would you escort me there?"

He silently congratulated her on her recovery. This was a resilient young woman. "Delighted, Lady Aphrodite. It's an easy walk. My sister and her children are there. I'd like to introduce you." When he held out his arm, she placed her hand on it.

"Please tell me about them."

"Susannah has three children. The eldest, Geoffrey, is in his first year at Cambridge."

"Isn't that amazing," Aphrodite said as she strolled by his side, leaning slightly on his arm. "My brother Asklepios is also in his first year at Cambridge. I wonder if they know each other."

"If your brother is always in scrapes like Geoffrey, I would imagine they might be acquainted. I believe my nephew has recently been sent down, due to some prank or another. Susannah also has two daughters: Melissa is . . .

I'm not sure. I think she's about twelve. Maria may be eight or nine. I believe a few of Frederick's friends will be here, but I don't know which ones. Everyone looks forward to meeting you."

"And every-one of them knows about . . . oh, never mind. Please tell me about your family seat."

A very polite young woman, attempting to carry on a conversation when she must be overset, he thought, then began to tell her about Crusader's Cross, his family's historical estate.

After a short stroll, the path ended, and they had a clear view of the group assembled on the shore. Two laughing children and a young woman were in a boat paddled around an island by a young man. A woman sat on a blanket with two other young men, one wearing a brilliant green jacket. Standing close to the lake were several other people whom Aphrodite guessed to be her age or a little older.

"That's my sister Susannah. People say we look alike. The young scamp in shirtsleeves is my nephew Geoffrey. The other young man is the friend visiting him."

After they took a few more steps, Aphrodite stopped and put her hands on her cheeks. "What in the world is he doing here?" Then she ran across the uneven land toward the three on the blanket.

Asklepios! Aphrodite thought. But it couldn't be her brother Asklepios. Why would he be at Windwillow? Why wasn't he at Cambridge? Then the words of the viscount echoed in her ears.

Oh, no! Asklepios must have been sent down from Cambridge with Warwick's nephew. Her father would kill him. Although the high spirits and outrageous larks of his children usually delighted the Marquis, he did not tolerate anything that interrupted their education.

"Ask—," she began. Before she could complete the name, the young man in the startling green jacket turned around to look at her. Aphrodite swallowed her word in surprise. Not only was her brother wearing a hideous jacket, but his light brown hair was curled. Tied around the riotous locks he wore a green and red band. His face paled when he saw his sister.

"Buon giorno," he shouted when she stopped and stared at him. "And who-a is this-a *bella* lady?"

She blinked. "What in the world . . . ?" she began.

The other young man leaped to his feet. "Good day. And how are you today?"

Asklepios strode toward Aphrodite and held out his hand. "Don't say a word. We'll explain later," he whispered. *"Bella, bella, bella,"* her brother said loudly as he took her hand, bowed, and feigned a kiss on it. "Please," he begged in a whisper, "please don't give me away."

"I am Geoffrey Hamilton, Warwick's nephew." The young man nodded. "This is my friend, the Conti di Versanti. He's from Italy."

Asklepios tapped his heels together and nodded his head, the ends of the band around his head flipping up and down with the motion.

"Yes, Geoffrey. How pleasant to meet you. I am Lady Aphrodite Herrington."

"Lady Aphrodite, we didn't expect you so early." Geoffrey swallowed.

"That is obvious."

"I am Susannah, Warwick's sister and Geoffrey's mother. So happy to have you here, Lady Aphrodite."

She turned to accept the hand Susannah Hamilton held out. "I am so pleased to meet you, Lady Susannah. Your brother has told me about you and your family."

"He believes we are a band of ruffians. You must not believe a word my brother says, although they are often true. We have descended upon Frederick so we could meet you and are so rag-mannered that we brought two extra guests."

"Unexpected guests. They were sent down for the remainder of the summer, as I understand," Warwick said.

"I have met the conti before," Aphrodite said. "If you don't mind." She included Susannah and Warwick in her glance. "I would like to chat with him for a moment. To ask him about his family."

"His family back in Italy," Geoffrey said with a grin and a nod.

"Certainly, Lady Aphrodite," Susannah said. "There is a gazebo just up there." She pointed toward a small summer house. "It will afford you some shade and privacy."

"Thank you." Aphrodite glared at her brother, forcing him to follow her. "We shall not be long." She smiled at the group as she shoved a lagging Asklepios ahead of her.

When she had settled herself in the gazebo, she frowned at Asklepios and demanded, "What are you doing? Were you sent down?"

"Not exactly." He refused to meet her eyes.

"Well, what happened and how did you end up the conti of whatever?"

"Wasn't that an inspiration, Ditie?" His face lit up with joy.

"Aski, I want an explanation."

"It was a prank, although it was for an interest that burns within me." Aski thumped his chest and stared out of the gazebo like a martyr, allowing her a view of his pensive profile. The Herringtons were inclined to strike poses that showed them at their best. "You know how much I love medicine. I want to study a body but I'm too young. The unjustness of society."

"Aski." Aphrodite's voice took on a forceful, no-nonsense tone.

"Oh, the prejudice that turned anatomical study into a crime," Aski continued. He ignored the interruptions and pounded himself on the chest again.

"Aski, resurrectionists have not been imprisoned for years. Just tell me exactly why you are here."

"Alas, I am a scholar with an interest in healing the body but, because I'm only . . ."

"Answer my question," Aphrodite said in a determined voice.

Aski turned and finally met his sister's eyes. "I heard that a dog had died and the family buried him. Geoffrey—he's the best of all fellows, Ditie—he and I decided to dig him up so I could dissect him."

"That doesn't sound so terrible, Aski. What happened?"

"The dog belonged to the magistrate's daughter."

"Oh, Aski, no!"

"And he found us digging it up at midnight."

"Aski!" She covered her mouth with her hands and leaned forward. "What happened then?"

"He chased us out of the yard. He was shooting at us, Ditie. We knew he'd come to the university to look for us, so we decided it was best to play least in sight. We told the proctor that Geoff's mother wrote us and we had to attend this house party because of the joining of our two families."

"You knew I was coming here?"

"Of course, Ditie. Everyone in Geoff's family knows you're here. All of society knows. And they know why."

Aphrodite groaned.

"Geoffrey's family is worried because it seems that Mrs. Horne is the most horrible person. We decided we'd better get away from Cambridge because the magistrate's daughter was upset. One of our friends who lives close to the magistrate said she really loved this dog and having him dug up distressed her."

"I can certainly understand her feelings, but why are you pretending to be the conti?" She leaned back in preparation for the convoluted reasoning common to the other Herringtons.

"I couldn't tell Papa, Ditie. You know that."

And she did. Their father directed a gaze on any of his erring children that made even Aphrodite regret a misstep he did not find amusing. Aski had met it often before.

"I thought Papa would be here, and I didn't have any place else to go. I couldn't explain to him, Ditie, you know that."

She nodded.

"Where else could I stay? All my friends are still in school, and our relatives would have told Papa that I was visiting them. So, I disguised myself as this Italian for a few days of freedom."

"Why as an Italian?" She followed his reasoning but not his conclusion.

"Lord, Ditie, it's a lark. Just a lark." He rolled his eyes. "Anyway, I planned to get sick, just pretend to, before you arrived, then stay in my room until we could figure out what to do. As Geoff said, we didn't expect you until much later."

"Aski, have you ever seen an Italian?" Aphrodite asked.

"No, but I think I look bang up." He patted his hair and straightened the green jacket.

"Have you ever spoken to an Italian?"

"No, but Geoff's aunt once had an Italian dance master, and Geoff told me all about him."

"How did you get your hair so curly?" She stood to pat his ringlets and watched them spring back from her touch.

"I put it in papers every night. I swear, I don't understand how you girls can sleep in those things. They hurt." He rubbed his scalp.

"And the ribbons around your head?"

"That was my idea. Geoff said that Italians are flamboyant. I thought they made the disguise more authentic," he said with a toss of his head.

"Italians don't wear bands on their heads, Aski. You're thinking of the Romany. They tie ribbons around their heads and carry tambourines." Her voice became so loud that when she turned to look at the group on the shore, she saw they were looking toward the summer house.

"You look absurd," she said in quiet tones. "You're not fooling anyone."

'Ditie, I've fooled *everyone*." He waved gaily toward the others. "Geoff's the only person here who knows—and you, now, of course. Don't give me away, Ditie."

Aphrodite looked at the party on the shore. They were sneaking covert looks at them, wondering about the length and the animation of the conversation between Lady Aphrodite and her old family friend, an attractive young man. Hardly the behavior of a woman who had come here to meet the mother of the man she might soon marry. It was time to return to the others.

"Meet me tonight so we can talk about this more. On the steps in front of the house at midnight." She started to leave the summer house.

"Ditie, did Mama and Papa arrive with you?" For a moment his flamboyant attitude changed. He looked like a frightened eighteen-year-old.

"You don't have to worry about Papa's anger for a while. Mama and Papa have gone to the country."

"Why didn't they come with you, Ditie?"

"Why do you think, brother?"

"Not again!"

"I guess so." Aphrodite whispered as she moved away, "Please, Aski, stop this ridiculous deception and be yourself, just be a guest."

"Don't you understand, Ditie? I can't. Someone will tell

Papa, or it will get back to the magistrate that I'm here. We're not that far from school."

"For heaven's sake, Aski, no one would tell Papa that you're here. You don't want to shed the disguise because you're having such a wonderful time."

The words could be the motto of the Mad Herringtons: *I'm having great fun. Don't interrupt an adventure.*

Chapter Five

Mrs. Horne hunched over the table, dripping gravy on her stained white ruffles and dribbling wine down her immense chest. On her right sat Aphrodite, the guest of honor, to Mrs. Horne's left was Warwick. Frederick faced his mother at the other end of the table. On Aphrodite's left was Fothergill, a quiet young man who ate silently.

On each side sat ten guests. At the far end, close to Frederick, sat Asklepios. Next to him, sat the squire's younger daughter Elsie, a vivacious dark-haired miss not even out of the schoolroom. Aski flirted with her outrageously. When he flung his head back, the ribbons danced and the spangles bounced and glittered.

Four chairs down the table from her sat Terpsi, another problem. Aphrodite's unconventional sister stared at Warwick with a smoldering gaze. The viscount, however, pretended he didn't see her, chatting with his dinner partner or drawing Mrs. Horne's attention from Aphrodite with a question.

Terpsi later changed her tactic by flirting with the gentleman to her right, a Mr. Hugh Ridley, a friend of Mr.

Horne's since childhood. A pleasant young man, a little plump but amiable and with a lovely estate in Sussex.

Terpsi's neckline dipped to such an immodest depth that Aphrodite feared her sister's breasts would tumble out. Although most of the men at the table watched the delicate balancing act with rapt attention, Warwick kept his eyes firmly fixed on the head of the table and disregarded the signals Terpsi hurled toward him.

When she realized Aphrodite watched her, Terpsi rolled her eyes toward Aski and smiled. Aphrodite knew her sister thought the Italian disguise was a marvelous lark and would never say a word to their parents.

At least Athena was behaving herself. She was five seats to the right of Warwick and recognized the futility of attracting him at such a distance. Nor had she noticed Aski. After an unfortunate experience with the son of an impoverished French noble, she had little romantic interest in foreigners.

After she ascertained that her family would not cause too much embarrassment, Aphrodite turned to her hostess. She discovered that conversation with Mrs. Horne was impossible. The older woman slurped her soup and tore her meat from the bone with her teeth. When she saw a morsel she coveted on Aphrodite's plate, she impaled it on her fork and shoved it in her mouth, chewing in open-mouthed satisfaction.

"Who's that foreigner down there making such a cake of himself with Newton's daughter?" Mrs. Horne demanded of Warwick.

"I don't know him well. A friend of Susannah's son Geoffrey," he answered. "However, I believe Lady Aphrodite is acquainted with him."

"Who is he, girl?"

"He's from Italy."

"Ah, an Italian. No wonder." With that, Mrs. Horne returned to her food.

When Aphrodite turned to Fothergill, her dinner partner on the left, Mrs. Horne pounded on the table with her fist and said, "Girl, tell me about your family again." And Aphrodite did, beginning to think of it as a nursery rhyme or a bedtime story. Indeed, the third time the crone demanded it, Mrs. Horne fell asleep with a spoonful of pudding halfway to her mouth before Aphrodite had even mentioned her brother Ares.

Aphrodite blinked and looked across the table where Warwick smiled and nodded, then pretended to fall asleep with his head dangerously close to his pudding. She bit her lips to keep from bursting out in thoroughly impolite laughter.

This is awkward, Aphrodite thought, attempting to be mature and kind. Poor woman, she'll be mortified when she realizes she was snoring in front of her guests.

Aphrodite reached out a hand to awaken her when the viscount whispered, "No, don't. She always does this."

Aphrodite finished her gooseberry cream to the roar of Mrs. Horne's snores.

"Doesn't she have a wonderful hearty appetite?" Frederick came around the table. "Mother, the ladies are ready to adjourn to the parlor."

Mrs. Horne hoisted herself from the chair and, between two footmen, led the ladies to the parlor while the gentlemen finished their port. As Aphrodite left the room, she saw that Athena had not left with the ladies but with a smug grin had settled in the chair next to Warwick. With a sigh, Aphrodite returned to the dining room, took her sister by the hand, and dragged her toward the parlor.

"How could you dare stay with the gentlemen? The only female there! Athena, you behave like a wanton," Aphrodite whispered.

"What's wrong with being a wanton?" Athena demanded and pulled back on Aphrodite's hand like a spoiled donkey. "I like men."

Aphrodite stopped. If Athena didn't know what was wrong with being a wanton, she hadn't the least notion of how to explain it. Instead, she grabbed Athena's arm even more tightly and towed her down the hall.

As they entered the parlor, Aphrodite pushed Athena toward the two girls her age and looked around for Terpsi. When she spied her sister alone in a dim corner, Aphrodite sat down next to Terpsi. "Have you talked to Athena yet?" she demanded.

"Dear sister, I haven't had time. I didn't realize when we spoke that you would rush into this engagement and drag us off to this terrible woman's house. I promise that I will talk to our sister."

"Soon?"

"Yes, Ditie, soon. Now, did you wonder why I have settled myself in this secluded corner? It was not to talk to you. I'm waiting for Warwick and wish you would leave so he and I can have a private *tête-à-tête.*" She leaned back in the chair and arranged her robe.

"But I have something to tell you, about Asklepios," Aphrodite persevered.

"Not now." Terpsi shooed Aphrodite away. "Warwick has just come in."

Aphrodite stood to move toward Susannah, but Warwick ignored Terpsi's gauche waves and winks and took Aphrodite's hand. "Lady Aphrodite, could we continue our unfinished conversation of this afternoon?" He led her toward two chairs as far from the fire and Mrs. Horne as could be found.

Aphrodite looked over her shoulder where Athena and Terpsi glared at her. She shrugged and returned her attention to Warwick. "Of course, my lord. I wasn't aware that we had not completed it."

He allowed her to sit, then moved the other chair closer. "You were so deep in thought when we returned to the house that I didn't get to ask you. You seemed to be delighted and a little surprised to see the conti. Is he an old acquaintance?"

"Yes, he is." She paused for a long time. Good heavens, what should she say? "I've known him for many years."

"How many years?" he queried.

"Oh, since he was a child. I even know his parents. They are like family to me."

"Ah. Did you meet him in Italy?"

"No, no. He's often been to our estate."

"And how did your family become acquainted with him?"

"I really don't know. My parents met him when I was but a child." So far she hadn't lied, but she couldn't let him know that the conti was her brother. How would she ever explain that to Frederick and his mother? How could she explain it to Warwick, the head of their family? Blast the Mad Herringtons. She was always the one left to clean up after their escapades.

"He's a handsome young man, don't you agree?" The viscount leaned forward as he spoke. His eyes held a glitter she didn't understand.

"Yes, very handsome."

"But, certainly his coloring is unusual for an Italian. Most are quite dark, and yet the conti has light hair and fair skin."

"Yes, that's not unusual, in his region of Italy." Oh, dear, the prevarication had begun.

He leaned closer to her, his lips so near her ear she could smell the scent he used. Spicy, a little sharp, but very pleasant. More than pleasant. She had trouble concentrating on his question.

"He dresses eccentrically. I didn't realize Italians dressed like that."

She saw that sparkle in his eye, again. Certainly he wasn't laughing, was he?

"I believe they do," Aphrodite said. "He always wore bright colors when he visited us." She looked down at her lap where her fingers fidgeted, pleating the embroidered cambric of her dress. She folded her hands in her lap.

"And the ribbons around his head?"

"Oh, yes." She felt such a fool. His lips twitched. He knew she was lying, but she had to carry on with the charade. "I believe the ribbons are part of the . . . um, traditional national costume, from his region of Italy."

"I have visited Italy and never saw that style before. What part of Italy is he from?"

"It's a very small region in the mountains. No one goes there. It's through a very narrow and dangerous pass. The . . . Vertotsi Pass. His people lead very isolated lives and are suspicious of outsiders." She was breathless from the effort of so many lies. She wasn't good at this. Would the interrogation never end?

"And yet, suspicious as the family was, they allowed him to leave this isolated valley, to visit your family in England?"

Her brain was becoming tangled. What had she said? "Oh, yes. My grandfather was a friend of his . . . of his great-uncle, whom he rescued from an accident in the mountains. And so they have always trusted our family."

"Oh, I see." Warwick leaned back in the chair, and Aphrodite relaxed in relief. "I thought he said he was Conti di Versanti, and yet you said the Vertotsi Pass. Was it not named for the family?"

She had thought the interrogation over and had relaxed

too soon. "Oh, you must forgive me. My Italian is atrocious. My tongue always gets tangled with all those vowels, and I never use his title. I always call him . . ." She stopped and searched her memory for an Italian name. "I call him Luigi."

"Then if you are being informal with your friends, may I ask you to call me Thomas?"

"Oh, I'm informal only with Luigi. We've known him so long. My parents met him years ago so he's . . . he's like a brother to me."

"How fortunate that your parents were able to make his acquaintance, when he lives in such an isolated part of Italy."

"Yes, fortunate." Aphrodite looked over her shoulder. Where were her sisters when she needed them?

"How, exactly, did they meet?"

Had she answered the question earlier? She couldn't remember. She glanced at Warwick and surprised a smile, which he hastily stifled. "How, exactly, did they meet?" she repeated.

"Yes," he repeated. "How exactly did they meet?"

Oh, she knew she'd answered this before, but the fabrications were running together in a brain overwhelmed by his presence and the unaccustomed strain of lying. She did it terribly, and she could tell by the look of irreverent amusement Warwick wore that he didn't believe a word she said. "Oh, yes, my grandfather . . ."

Aphrodite never thought she'd be glad to see Terpsi but when her sister swooped down on them, Aphrodite leaped to her feet.

"I was wondering—" Warwick stood as Aphrodite attempted to excuse herself. "My Italian is not good, but thought the word for "count" is *conte*, not *conti*."

"I believe in his region of Italy . . ."

"Ah, yes, that isolated region again."

Terpsi took Warwick's arm and smiled up at him with a shake of her head. "Certainly the conti knows his own title."

Aphrodite hurried away from him, delighted to leave him with Terpsi, who could handle fabrication so much more easily than she.

Drat the man! He knew something about Asklepios was havey-cavey. Well, so would anyone with any brain, but the others were politely accepting the fiction. She looked back over her shoulder and Warwick winked at her. The man had no manners.

She started toward Athena, but her younger sister's eyes flashed as she stared at Warwick and Terpsi. Her mouth was a straight line. Well aware that this signaled an anger Aphrodite wasn't willing to provoke, she looked for another chair.

Mrs. Horne beckoned to her, thumping the floor with her stick and shouting, "Girl!"

Oh, please, no, she said to herself. In answer to her supplication, a hand grasped hers and pulled her down on a bench against the wall.

"Please, won't you sit with me?" Susannah asked. "Now that you're about to join the family, I'd love to get to know you. Tell me all about yourself."

Aphrodite felt at ease enough to say, "I wonder if I might ask you a question? There is something that confuses me."

"Of course. Whatever could it be?"

"I had thought that Frederick was an only child because his mother was not able to have more children. I've heard she wanted more. Perhaps she lost some children at birth?"

"Oh, no. It is my understanding that after Frederick was conceived, Uncle Bernard was pleased to have an heir and Aunt Matilda felt she had done her duty. Well, they decided not to . . . oh, how do I say this? They decided to have no more children."

"Oh." Aphrodite considered this. "Is that possible?"

"Yes, although I can see how that might surprise you," Susannah said in a gentle voice.

"How did they do that?" Aphrodite wondered aloud.

"Oh, dear. This is difficult to explain to an unmarried woman. They decided not to . . . not to . . . be in the same bed together."

"People do that?" Aphrodite's voice went up an octave.

With a laugh, Susannah answered, "Not in all families, but, yes, within a marriage of convenience it is not uncommon."

"Girl, come here."

Aphrodite could no longer ignore the summons, especially with Frederick standing next to her and holding out his arm.

"Please excuse me," she said to Susannah and turned toward the white toad. Could she live with her? She banished the question for the moment in the hope she could find something to like in Frederick's mother.

"Your family's strange," Mrs. Horne said. "Look at that oddly dressed chit over there, flaunting herself at Warwick."

Aphrodite couldn't refute the statement. "I believe she finds him very attractive. Now, Mrs. Horne, why don't you tell me about Frederick when he was young? I would love to know more about him."

"All women find Warwick attractive. Don't the girl know he's seen more flesh than my chef? I don't know why the girls flock to him. I don't know what he's looking for, but flesh ain't it." Mrs. Horne emphasized each of the last words with a nod of her head and the thump of her cane.

"Mrs. Horne, I imagine Frederick was a darling child. Do tell me . . ."

"And that younger sister. What's her foolish name?" She waved her cane toward the group of young women.

"Do you mean my dear sister Athena?"

"That's the one. Yella-headed chit. Nothing inside, is there? More hair than wit."

She fixed a cold stare on the woman. "I am very fond of my family, Mrs. Horne."

"Glad to hear that. Family loyalty is important. Must be difficult for you. They're wild to a fault. Frederick tells me you're not like the rest of your family."

When she heard the words she had often spoken come from the white toad's mouth, Aphrodite felt deep shame. She looked up at her betrothed, who stood behind his mother's chair and listened to the conversation without a word. "We are different in some ways, Mrs. Horne, but I do love my family and do not like to hear anyone speak ill of them," she said slowly.

"Come, Mother, let us think of another topic of conversation that is more to Lady Aphrodite's liking." Frederick leaned down between the women. "Perhaps you could tell her about your lovely gardens."

"I want to go to bed," Mrs. Horne said as she struggled to her feet. "Everyone, continue what you're doing." She waved as she shuffled toward the door on her son's arm.

Aphrodite had sent Mignon away without having her help her out of her dress, then sat with a shawl wrapped around her on the window seat of her chambers and looked out at the dark garden below her.

Goodness, she was tired. And no wonder, after this day. First she had met Frederick's esteemed mother, the woman she'd hoped to love. She'd discovered instead a terrible, crude harridan she was doomed to live with for the rest of her life.

Then, she had spent time with Warwick. He'd behaved properly but always seemed to be laughing at her. Why? And flirting with her as well. She knew better than to lose her head over him. Even Mrs. Horne had warned the Herringtons away from him. Certainly Aphrodite herself had had enough experience with his uncertain ways to know better.

He'd been kind earlier today, after she'd met Mrs. Horne. She knew he wasn't interested in her, not as a woman. It was more of a game for him. He wasn't the marrying sort. Was he getting to an age when he should think about setting up his nursery? Would he marry Terpsi? Aphrodite didn't think so. Terpsi was too forward even for him. Athena? He had said she was lovely and young. Didn't most men want a young bride they could shape to their wills and who would give them children? Certainly the latter was a Herrington characteristic greatly in demand.

Warwick was handsome. Aphrodite had never seen a man so handsome, an opinion she shared with both of her sisters and most of the females of the *ton*. His eyes twinkled at the most inappropriate times, even at moments when she didn't realize there was anything amusing happening until he invited her to share the fun.

This evening he had shown a preference for her, but, after all, what were his choices at this house party? Terpsi, Athena, the two other young girls of Athena's age, the wives of relatives and friends, and she, Aphrodite. And she was almost betrothed. A light flirtation was out of the question for a woman in her position. Not that she'd carry on any kind of dalliance, as Warwick knew. Flirtation was a talent the other Herringtons had been born with, but she hadn't inherited it.

She looked out the window again. The moon had risen and bathed the grounds in a faint light. She could tell that Aski had not yet appeared.

No, she wasn't like the other Herrington women.

In her first season, Warwick had courted her. For a fortnight, he showed great interest in her. He'd taken her for rides in the park, stood up with her at Almack's, danced with her at every party. In fact, he'd carefully discovered which parties she and her family were attending so he could meet her there.

One night, when the air was heavy with the scent of lavender, he'd led her to the garden. They had held hands and, without speaking, walked together through the curving paths. She had felt a tension she didn't understand, a delightful yearning for something she knew lay ahead. Then he'd stopped and she looked up into his face as he lifted her chin. His eyes were soft and gentle but also glittering with an emotion she couldn't define. Then he kissed her. A light, sweet kiss. The only kiss she'd ever received on the lips, a kiss which raised such a hunger within her that she understood the intensity of the attraction between her mother and father, and she craved it.

When the kiss was over, she stood on her toes, reaching up for another, but he said, "Not now, little one." Then he had placed her hand on his arm and covered it with his other hand, leading her back through the garden with tenderness and care.

Tonight, as she looked out the window, she thought of the bench she and Warwick had shared only hours earlier. She stood, rubbing her hands, desperate to forget the passion that had overwhelmed her with the long-ago kiss.

Poor, innocent child that I was, she thought. She'd believed the kiss meant he loved her, that they were betrothed. She had dreamed of a wedding in St. James, her younger sisters as her bridesmaids and herself, glowing and beautiful, for once the center of attention as she came down the aisle toward her beloved.

But the next night, she'd been walking in a garden with another young man. She saw Warwick in the rose garden, kissing Leticia Brightonby in exactly the same way he had kissed her, but Leticia, the strumpet, leaned against his body, and he wrapped his arms around her.

Aphrodite had stood completely still, watching, wishing she'd leaned against his hard strength. She realized she was clutching her escort's arm only when he exclaimed in pain and attempted to pry her fingers away. She loosened her grasp but couldn't let go, fearing she'd fall without his support. She couldn't stop watching as Warwick smiled down at Leticia. Aphrodite knew that smile. She believed it had been only for her alone. It was just one of his many charms. Lord, she felt like such a fool!

When she could finally move, she took a step forward, then twirled around on her escort's arm and headed back to the party, pulling him along behind her. Once inside the ballroom, she chattered and danced and smiled as she never had before. Never let it be said that a Herrington displayed her broken heart to the world.

The betrayal and her own guileless stupidity hurt so much she never wanted to see him again. She nodded but turned away when he approached her at musical evenings or in the park. At balls, she danced with him and was pleasant to him at Terpsi's literary gatherings, but only because she refused to make a scene in society. Herringtons had done that far too often.

She wouldn't think about it anymore. With great effort, she wrenched her thoughts to another subject.

What was she going to do with Athena? The chit was so forward she would be ruined. If she saw nothing wrong with being a wanton, Mama would just have to talk with her. Mama was certainly not a wanton.

Terpsi. There was nothing she could do with her either. Independent all her life, she would not listen to Aphrodite or anyone else.

And Aski—how was she going to solve that problem? She looked at the clock. It was almost midnight. She rose, walked to the door, and opened it. Looking both ways, she saw that the hall was empty. Not that anyone in this house party would indulge in the immoral activities that she'd heard took place at many others. She tiptoed out of her chambers, closed the door silently behind her, and trod quietly down the stairs and across the marble floor of the entry, where she waited and paced.

Twenty minutes passed before Aski joined her. Without speaking, she pulled him to the door, opened it, and dragged him around the house to sit on the bench where she had rested that afternoon.

"Aski, this is the most inane scrape you've ever been in. You look foolish."

"I think I look handsome and dashing," he said with the Herrington's customary lack of humility. Then he patted his hair and straightened the green jacket. "The squire's daughter was impressed."

"Everyone knows you're not Italian. A foolish accent, curly hair, and a ribbon are not a disguise. Now, why don't you stop this ridiculous deception and just be a guest?"

"I told you. I can't. If Papa finds out . . . well, you know what he'll do. Or if it gets around the neighborhood that I'm here, the magistrate might hear. We're not that far from school." He flipped the ribbons on his head again. "Don't worry, Ditie. It'll be all right. We'll hide here for ten more days. When we get back to Cambridge, the magistrate will have forgotten all about it."

"But Terpsi or Athena might give you away if I don't."

"Athena hasn't even noticed I'm here. I'll wager Terpsi thinks it's a lark. She's a game one. She'll help me."

"Right now she's somewhat distracted." She stood and tried one more time. "Aski, you still look like yourself. When you go to London next year for the season, everyone here is going to recognize you. What are you going to say?"

"I don't know." He shrugged. "I'll decide that if someone asks. Right now, I'm having fun." He looked down at her, then put his arm around her shoulder and held her. "You worry too much. Just relax and enjoy yourself."

"By the way, your name is Luigi. At least, that's what I told Warwick it was."

"Luigi," he repeated. "Luigi." He rolled the name over his tongue. "Luigi. Yes, I like it. I *am* Luigi."

Then he kissed her on the cheek. "Go on and get some sleep. See you in the morning."

Nothing made her feel less like a Herrington than a conversation like this.

Warwick couldn't sleep. Every time he closed his eyes, two Herringtons came toward him, smiling and fluttering eyelashes. One had pale blond hair and the other held the neckline of her dress with one hand. In the background stood the quiet one with flushed cheeks. The one almost betrothed to his cousin. The one who most definitely should not be appearing in his dreams.

He pulled the sheet up to his neck and turned, pulling the pillow over his eyes because the moon was so bright. Minutes later, his eyes were still wide open and he was no closer to sleep. With an oath, he threw the pillow on the floor, tossed the covers back, stomped around the room, then looked out the window.

The full moon reflected off the lake and filled the entire landscape with light. As he watched the water, he became aware that someone was below him, in the clearing where the bench overlooked the lake. He could make out two figures engaged in an lively discussion. The man threw his arms in the air while the woman sat still on the bench. Then she stood and walked toward him, leaning forward as if she were shouting, until the man put his arm around her and she snuggled next to him. When the man kissed her, Warwick thought he should turn away from the tryst, but the encounter seemed oddly passionless. Finally, the woman turned away and came toward the house.

As she approached the house and passed beneath his window, the moonlight shone on her face. Aphrodite Herrington. *My, my,* he thought as she went toward the front door.

Who was the man? Would Frederick have met with his betrothed at midnight? Was his cousin more romantic than he'd thought? Dear Matilda wouldn't approve. But when the masculine figure passed under the window, he recognized the curly locks of the man who called himself Luigi Versasi. Or Versani. He wasn't really sure of the name either.

Warwick fell back on the bed. Who was this young man Aphrodite met alone at midnight and allowed to kiss her? He began to imagine many scenarios but none fit the Aphrodite Herrington he was acquainted with. Curious, he shrugged into his robe and stepped into the hallway. He knew which wing housed the Herringtons and snuck along the shadowed corridor until he could look down its length. Aphrodite tiptoed across the carpet and into her room. At the other end of the hall, a figure entered the room next to Geoff's and closed the door.

What was going on? Warwick grinned.

Midnight assignations, mysterious foreigners, the Mad Herringtons. Lord, this was going to be fun!

Chapter Six

When had she lost any semblance of control over her siblings? Aphrodite wondered. She sipped a cup of chocolate and contemplated her reflection in the mirror as Mignon brushed and smoothed her hair into a confection of curls and braids.

When they were younger, Terpsi, Athena, and Aski had been impulsive and audacious but fairly well behaved. Now Athena and Terpsi had burst into womanhood like orchids in a greenhouse, and she had no idea how to fend off the swarm of men drawn to them.

She closed her eyes and tried to think of something more pleasant, something she could take care of, but a vision of a wingéd Warwick leading that swarm hovered on the edge of her consciousness.

And Aski. Was there anything more foolish than this Italian nobleman escapade? Well, he wasn't hurting anyone, and she could only hope it wouldn't embarrass the family. Hah! she thought. As if anything he could do would discomfit anyone but her.

"There you are, Lady Aphrodite." Mignon stepped back

and looked at her mistress in the mirror. "If you didn't have those frown lines, you'd look a fair treat."

Startled, Aphrodite stared in the mirror at herself. Yes, she did have frown lines, deep ones between her eyebrows.

"I'll find some white lily water, Lady Aphrodite. That should smooth out your lovely skin with no problem. You do have lovely skin, my lady. Prettiest in your family."

"Thank you, Mignon." Aphrodite rose and smoothed down the skirt of her deep blue morning dress. The color did bring out the auburn shade in her hair and showed her creamy skin to the best advantage. All in all, she did look rather well, she thought. Certainly no one would notice those deep lines etched by worry.

"What's bothering you this morning, fair Patience?" Warwick sat alone in the breakfast parlor. He put down the newspaper and stood as she entered. "Did you not sleep well last night?" He thought her lovely skin looked a trifle pale this morning. There were lines on her forehead, and purple smudges seemed to have permanently settled beneath her eyes. Had she been up too late with that Italian? Had she been unable to sleep? He could not tell her that she looked fagged out, but he was concerned.

She rubbed her fingers across the lines. "Oh, dear. Are they that noticeable?" She laughed. "I must look like a hag."

But she wasn't really laughing. There was a quaver in her voice he'd never noticed before, and it troubled him. She was worried, obviously so. Warwick reached out, placed her hand on his arm, and led her to a chair. Once she was settled, he poured her a cup of tea.

"Would you like sugar?" He handed her the cup.

"Thank you. This is just how I like my tea." She sipped it and leaned back in the chair in contentment.

"I'm afraid we are alone this morning. My sister and her brood are eating in the nursery."

"And I'm sure my sisters are still in bed."

"Frederick always eats late, with his revered mother, and my nephew and your Italian friend went off early this morning for some adventure."

"Oh, dear." She sighed as she straightened, and the lines between her lovely eyes deepened. "What could they be up to?"

"You know how boys are."

"Only too well." There was a touch of stoic acceptance in her voice.

"May I get you some breakfast?"

"I'm perfectly capable of getting—"

"There is no doubt in my mind that you are capable, but you might take advantage of having someone wait on you for a change."

"What a luxury," Aphrodite said with a charming laugh. "Then fill my plate up with whatever looks good. I do like haddock and buttered eggs."

When he placed two plates in front of her, she smiled up at him. How little it takes to please her, he thought.

"Oh, my lord, you must think I have my brothers' appetites. Will you not share this plate?"

"You are entirely too thin, my lady. I believe we shall have to fatten you up. Isn't that why one comes to the country? To regain one's health and vitality?"

"I had hoped the country would be restoring." The frown threatened again. "However, it has been a little more taxing than I expected."

"Are your sisters giving you trouble again, dear Patience?"

"I am certainly not Patience, nor do I need another name. Aphrodite is name and enough."

"Then may I use it, since, after all, we are to be family. You must call me Thomas, as I have requested before."

"You insist, Thomas?"

He was surprised at how easily she had finally accepted the suggestion. Probably due to lower resistance, with all the capers her siblings indulged in. "Yes, please call me Thomas. Now, tell me, what has you in the dismals? Could it be my Aunt Matilda, your sisters, and, perhaps, that young Italian scamp?"

"I scarce know what you mean. I love my family, and I am delighted to see Luigi again."

"Do not raise your hackles, my dear. If you are not ready to tell me, I shan't ask more. Know that I am a friend and do not like to see those lines of worry." He reached out and placed the index finger of his right hand on the bridge of her nose to smooth away the furrow.

When she jumped and looked frightened, he soothed her by saying, "I promise I will not harm you, but seeing you so anxious . . ." He stopped speaking because he had no idea how he felt, just that her distress greatly disturbed him. "I do not like to see you so anxious." He dropped his hand.

"Thank you. I appreciate your concern, but the thought of what could happen at any time with my dear family . . . well, the possibilities almost overwhelm me. I used to be quite good at taking care of my brothers and sisters, but, of late, I feel as if I have lost any influence I ever had."

"Surely you should not have to watch over them. Are they not grown?"

"Someone must, my lord."

"Thomas," he said and smiled.

"Thomas," she said and returned the smile. "I'm not sure that my siblings will ever be grown. There are so many of us that someone must be responsible."

"Surely that is the responsibility of your parents."

"I dearly love my parents and they love all of us, but

they have unusual ideas of how to rear children. They have allowed each child to experiment. This has led some into deep waters from which they must be rescued."

"But you are too young . . ."

"Someone," she said, and the lines between her eyes became deeper even as he watched. "*Someone* must make sure that Athe—that one of the girls doesn't blot her copy book or that one of the boys doesn't kill himself in a reckless prank."

At the entrance of a footman with hot tea, Warwick sat back in his chair and motioned for the servant to fill their cups. When he left, Warwick said, "But you are barely older than your sisters. Certainly it should be time for you to enjoy yourself."

"I am almost engaged, Thomas. There is no more time for fun." When she realized what she'd said, Aphrodite clapped her hands over her mouth. "Oh, dear, I didn't mean . . ."

"I'm sure you didn't." Warwick took one of her hands and held it. "Looking forward to a long life with the charming Matilda Horne must lead to paroxysms of joy." As she studied the other hand, which now lay in her lap, Warwick said, "I wish I could assume part of your burden, my dear, but it is obvious you are not going to allow that. I will vex you no longer. Do tell me what you hear from your older brother Aeolus. He and I often discussed his obsession with the Nile when we were in school together."

"We hear nothing, but that is not unusual. Aeolus has never been much of a correspondent. Even as a child, he shut himself up and read books about science and distant places. He actually caused little trouble, except, of course, for the time he fell off the west tower when he pretended to be climbing the Himalayas. Or the time he was searching for the Northwest Passage and almost drowned in Mama's lily pond. Actually, he was much less bother than Aski . . .

than my other brothers." She stopped, glanced at him then away, and took a deep breath before continuing. "Did you ever meet my sister Artemis? I believe she came out . . ."

"My first year in town. She was lovely to look at but already in love with Sanderson so the rest of us just admired her and fought to sign her dance card." He paused for a moment, allowing her to believe that her sudden change of subject had caused him to forget what she obviously considered a slip. "And how old is your brother Aski?"

"Much younger than I am." She dabbed at her mouth with her napkin then stood. "I must hurry. Just in case my sisters need me. I will need to check on what . . . on what they are wearing."

"Do they not have dressers?"

"Oh, yes, but they depend on me. To tell them what to wear. And other things. Excuse me." She almost ran from the room.

So she had a scamp of a younger brother named Aski. He'd ask Susannah if she'd ever heard Geoffrey talk about him.

"Isn't the garden lovely this time of year?" Frederick asked Aphrodite, who held his right arm, then turned to Athena to extend his left.

Athena held up the skirt of her fetching pale blue morning gown to keep it from picking up dirt or being torn by the ugly brown plants in Mrs. Horne's garden. She placed the matching shoes carefully, making sure that she did not step in mud or any other lurking menace in the squalid little garden.

Terpsichore strolled ahead of them, stopping to inspect the dwarf shrubs that stood in rows around the area.

"Lovely," answered Aphrodite.

"But why," Athena began, "why would anyone want a

garden with only brown and dark blue flowers and plants? Mama has the loveliest yellow roses. If one has to be in a garden, I prefer one with color."

"Everyone has different taste, Athena." Aphrodite paused by a bush that looked as if it had died years earlier after having been ravaged by insects and blight.

"Yes, Lady Athena." Mr. Horne gazed into Athena's large blue eyes. "My mother loves rare plants and trees that, perhaps, not everyone admires."

The four of them stood studying the array of hideous brown growth until the sound of a coach coming up the drive distracted them. They watched as a pair of matched bays pulled a black cabriolet to the front of the mansion. It was a plain carriage, without the adornment of nobility on the door, but well-kept and trim.

"Who can that be?" Aphrodite asked.

"Oh, no," Terpsi shrieked as a man climbed out of a coach. Eyes wide and breath coming in deep gasps, she turned to Mr. Horne. "Who is that?"

Mr. Horne looked up. "Why, that is my friend Callum McReynolds. I don't suppose you know him."

Aphrodite looked at her older sister. With her hands, Terpsi covered cheeks bleached of all color, then staggered to a bench and dropped on it.

"Yes, we do," Aphrodite answered when she realized that Terpsi could not speak. "I believe he and my sister Terpsichore met each other when she came out four years ago."

"How delightful. Callum is the best of all fellows. I'm happy he'll know someone here other than Mother and me."

"I don't believe he and Terpsi parted as friends," Aphrodite whispered.

Aphrodite wished she didn't have to mention this, but it was only fair to warn Frederick. The relationship between

Terpsi and Mr. McReynolds had been so volatile that it would soon be obvious to everyone in the house party they were not on the best of terms.

As his carriage disappeared around the drive and toward the stables, Callum McReynolds started up the steps only to be stopped by Mr. Horne's shout. McReynolds, a stocky man with thick, dark hair who dressed carelessly, his coat hanging from broad shoulders, turned and waved.

"Callum! Come over here. There are some people here I believe you know."

Aphrodite could see Mr. McReynold's broad smile when he saw Frederick and broke into a run.

"Frederick, how good to see you," he called as he approached. His voice still had the slight Scottish burr she remembered.

Callum stopped and looked at Aphrodite, then at Athena. A haunted look flashed across his face. He swallowed hard and searched the garden area with rapid glances. "Please tell me that your sister is not with you." He stopped talking when he saw Terpsi on the bench. She was huddled against a trellis, trying to make herself as small as possible, but he saw her nonetheless. After tossing his hat onto an emaciated bush, he covered his eyes with his hand before looking at Terpsi again.

"I'd hoped if I closed my eyes, you'd have disappeared by the time I opened them again," Mr. McReynolds said to Terpsi. "Alas, I was not so fortunate."

Stunned by his friend's rudeness, Mr. Horne put his hand on Callum's shoulder. "Come on, old friend. Certainly you don't mean that. I want you to meet Lady Aphrodite Herrington and her sisters, Lady Athena and Lady Terpsichore."

"I know the fair Herrington sisters," Mr. McReynolds said. "And that one," he nodded toward the bench. "Yes, that one only too well. How are you, Terpsi?"

"What a surprise to see you, Callum." Terpsi stood and strolled toward McReynolds, her back straight and her head held regally. "How long has it been? Three years? Four?"

"You witch, you know exactly . . ." He controlled himself with effort. "And your husband? Does he accompany you? I would like to console him on his choice of wives, if your tongue has not killed him yet."

Terpsi blanched, but she kept her head high. "I am not married. I have found more interesting pursuits than a life of *ennui* and servitude with one man."

He bowed. "All mankind thanks you."

Mr. Horne put a hand on his friend's arm. "Coming a little strong, Callum. Surely you can be polite to Lady Terpsichore after so many years and as my guest at this joyous occasion."

What sounded almost like a growl came from McReynolds, but he turned and thumped his hand on Mr. Horne's shoulder. "I am happy for you, but I think it would be better if I left."

"Please don't do that on my account," Terpsi said. "People might think you're running away. You do it so well."

McReynolds ignored the remark and turned to Aphrodite. "I had been invited to meet a special guest, but I did not know her identity. If you and Frederick are to be betrothed, I wish you both happiness. He is the best friend I have, and you were always pleasant to me." He turned and looked over his shoulder at Terpsi. "There are those in your family who were not."

"Now, if you will excuse me," he said to Frederick, "I will go in and wash off my dirt. We will talk later." With a nod to Athena and Aphrodite, he strode off.

"How interesting," Aphrodite murmured as McReynolds disappeared into the house, and Terpsi sank again onto a bench. Aphrodite turned toward her sister. "I knew that your relationship was turbulent, but I didn't realize it had ended so badly that he would be rude to you so many years later. He always seemed most pleasant and unexceptionable." When Terpsi did not answer, Aphrodite decided this was not the time to discuss the situation.

"Frederick, would you show Athena and me more of your mother's interesting garden while my sister recovers?"

Terpsi watched the three stroll across the dreary garden.

Memories overwhelmed her. Callum was the son of a manufacturer in Scotland and had attended Cambridge. It made sense that he and Mr. Horne knew each other. They had much in common.

Had she been in love with the man? Yes, head over heels! Recklessly so. She'd been willing to give everything up for him, but he had tossed her devotion in her face. Imagine, a middle-class man had rejected a Herrington. She gave a bark of laughter, but it held no amusement.

How long would he be here? Certainly through the week, unless he could think of an excuse to leave, but she didn't think he would. Not after her taunt.

She could do nothing. She couldn't leave. She was, after all, the chaperone for her two younger sisters, yet she wasn't sure she could be on the same estate with the man without sobbing or throwing herself at his feet.

On second thought, she would never let him know she had cried for him. Wouldn't he love knowing that? She raised her chin. Terpsichore Herrington had pride.

What right did he have to behave so rudely? It was as if he thought she had done something terrible. Well, if he were going to be rag-mannered, he would be the only one.

Terpsichore Herrington could take care of herself. Terpsichore Herrington could stand up to anyone or anything.

That evening when the guests gathered after dinner, Frederick organized card games for them.

"I have set up some small tables for those who would

like to play whist or piquet or ecarté. We could not find the Pope Joan board, but there is a large table for some of the younger guests who would like to play Speculation."

With great bravura, Terpsi stood and led Hugh Ridley to a table, where they sat and began a noisy game of piquet while Fothergill looked on.

Aphrodite looked around, wondering whom she should join, and saw Athena heading toward Warwick with a glimmer in her eyes and a sway in her walk. With a movement learned during many years of deflecting her siblings from inappropriate goals, she turned Athena toward the young people who had settled at the large round table to play Speculation. Once the scowling Athena was seated, Aphrodite again considered what she would do.

"Why don't you join us, Ditie?" Aski asked before he realized who he was supposed to be. "I mean-a, why don't you join us, pretty English lady?"

"Yes," Warwick said from behind her. "Why don't you join the young people, pretty English lady?"

She looked over her shoulder at him. His eyes still laughed at her attempts to treat her disreputable brother as an Italian noble. "Thank you. I believe I will. Do you join us?"

"I believe James wants to play piquet. You will excuse us, pretty English lady?"

The evening passed quickly. Terpsi shouted and laughed loudly to show Callum, who played cribbage with Frederick, that she was whole-hearted while Ditie, Athena, and the young people had a thoroughly delightful hour.

And through it all, Aphrodite was aware of Warwick's amused scrutiny of her and of Callum's refusal to look in Terpsi's direction.

Chapter Seven

The guests spent the next day in the usual house party activities. Frederick provided fine fishing for the gentlemen in a rushing river that crossed his land while the women took a pleasant walk to a nearby abbey. Athena's constant worry about the state of her clothing and loud complaints about long grass, dirt, rocks on the path, and low-hanging tree branches lessened the joy of the excursion somewhat for Aphrodite, but she enjoyed chatting with Susannah and the squire's wife.

That evening, Terpsi's voice interrupted the quiet camaraderie that had been growing among the guests and halted the friendly babble that filled the dark and over-heated parlor.

Terpsi rose only a few minutes after the gentlemen had joined the ladies. She shimmered in the gloom, her dark gold hair lose and curling over her shoulders and down her back. Her dress was of finest lawn with an exotic pattern of brilliant jade green, gold, and deep blue. Aphrodite be-lieved she'd never seen her sister looking so lovely, or so dangerous. She shivered, wondering what her unpredictable sister had in mind.

"If I may have your attention." Terpsi spoke in a husky tone that caused the men to move closer to her. Even Susannah's devoted husband, James, twisted in his chair so he could see Terpsi better. Frederick kept his position next to his mother, although he too leaned toward his future sister-in-law. Only Warwick and Callum acted unaware of her potent charms.

Mr. McReynolds sat next to Gwendolyn, the older of the squire's daughters, and chatted. For a moment, when Terpsi began to talk, Aphrodite could see him look up at her, his attention completely caught. Then he settled back in the chair, turned back toward Gwendolyn and continued his conversation, pretending absolute disinterest in Terpsi's actions.

Warwick settled in the chair next to Aphrodite, a hand touching her shoulder lightly for a moment before he dropped it into his lap and watched Terpsi.

Terpsi twirled, as if to look at those in the other end of the room, but Aphrodite knew that she was showing off the flow of her dress. And all the while, Terpsi watched Mr. McReynolds.

Callum was a nice-looking man, Aphrodite mused. His hair was shorter than was *à la mode*, nor was his coat fashionable. His features showed too much character to be considered handsome, but he was interesting, arresting, and memorable.

Aphrodite had always liked Callum. She'd thought he and Terpsi would marry. Terpsi adored him, and Aphrodite believed he loved her. Well aware of Terpsi's foibles, he never let her cut a wheedle around him. He would have been good for her.

What had happened? Aphrodite looked back and forth between the posturing Terpsi and the composed Callum.

When Callum had no longer called upon her, and she'd discovered that he had returned to Scotland without telling her, she lost her glorious vitality for weeks. Aphrodite had seen through the pretense immediately, as had even Athena and Aski, the most self-centered members of the family, but none dared to ask her. Terpsi had put on her most brilliant smile when Aphrodite attempted to talk to her and said, "La, it was nothing."

"Who would like to put on a play to entertain ourselves during the house party?" asked Terpsi.

"A play!" Susannah clapped and laughed. "What a wonderful idea. Just the thing to brighten our days."

"Do you have a play in mind?" James asked.

"I thought Mr. Shakespeare's *A Midsummer Night's Dream.*"

"Oh, I love that play!" Athena clapped and bounced on the sofa where she sat with Geoffrey. "It has fairies. I want to be in it."

"And so you shall. And so shall everyone who wishes to be." Terpsi looked at Callum for a moment. When he continued to talk with Gwendolyn, she said, "This is a play for any one who believes in magic and a love that lives eternally."

Terpsi threw the words at Callum. They echoed so loudly in the quiet that he was forced to turn and look at her, but his gaze froze her, so full was it of distaste and lack of interest. When he again leaned toward Gwendolyn, words gushed from Terpsi as if nothing had happened.

"Who would like to play what parts?" she asked.

"As if she hasn't already decided," Warwick whispered in Aphrodite's ear. His breath tickled and warmed her.

"You must play the part of Titania," Susannah said to Terpsi. "You are perfect for the Queen of the fairies."

"Thank you." Terpsi bowed. "I would enjoy that. I thought, perhaps my sisters could be Helena and Hermia.

Mr. Horne." She turned toward her future brother-in-law. "Perhaps you could be Demetrius to Aphrodite's Helena."

"That would be nice," Frederick said. "Won't this be fun, Mother?"

Mrs. Horne snored in response.

Terpsi paused as she looked around the room. "James and Susannah, will you be Theseus and Hippolyta?"

"How lovely. That's not a big part, so I can help with costumes and such," Susannah said.

"We'll have Geoffrey and the squire's sons, Hugh Ridley, and Fothergill play Quince, Bottom, and all those others." Terpsi dismissed them with a wave of her hand then added, "And Geoffrey's Italian friend shall make a perfect Puck."

Aski nodded back to her, then turned his attention to Elsie, the squire's other daughter.

"Who will play my dearest Oberon?" Terpsi wondered aloud.

When her eyes lit on Warwick, he said, "I believe I will be Lysander who is in love with Hermia." He bowed toward Athena.

"How lovely." Athena said. "I will like to be Hermia if you are Lysander."

"What?" said Terpsi, her voice sharp with disappointment. "Warwick, I thought you might wish to play Oberon. Well, then, who would like to play the part of Oberon?"

"Oh, Mr. McReynolds," Gwendolyn suggested. "He's ever so droll and certainly would be wonderful playing anyone. You don't have a part yet, do you, Mr. McReynolds?" She went off in a fit of giggles.

"Yes, I'll take part." Mr. McReynolds looked as if he'd sooner throw himself under a carriage. "Although I'm not much of an actor. Now, is there a part for my friend Miss Barlow?"

When Terpsi couldn't find an answer, Aphrodite suggested, "Perhaps Cobweb, one of the fairies?"

"Oh, yes. I shall dance and fly around." Gwendolyn clapped her hands and giggled again.

After all the parts were filled, Terpsi said, "Now, that's all settled. We will practice tomorrow." Her eyes sparkled, but not with joy. She returned to her chair between Hugh Ridley and Fothergill, back straight and chin high, her chest rising and falling with her deep breathing.

Aphrodite recognized the signs of anger in her sister but knew better than to say anything.

"How shall we learn our lines?" Warwick asked.

Terpsi rose again. "I packed some copies of a short version of the play, which I rewrote from the original. There should be enough for all of us to have a script. I shall hand them out tomorrow. When and where shall we rehearse?"

"The ballroom is perfect." Mr. Horne left his sleeping mother's side. "I can have the workmen build a stage." He pulled a chair over to sit next to Aphrodite.

"Then shall we meet there at eleven in the morning?" As the group agreed, Terpsi again sat and began an outrageous and masterful flirtation with both Fothergill and Hugh Ridley.

Aphrodite looked for the rest of her family. Athena fluttered her eyelashes at Geoffrey while Aski took little Elsie's hand. She giggled like her sister.

"I did want talk with you." Frederick said. "But it's been so long since I was able to sit with Mother."

"I understand." She understood one would wish to spend some time with one's mother, but she had hoped he'd also want to get acquainted with his future wife. Was this what marriage would be like? Coming in second to Frederick's mother? She feared it would be.

She turned toward Frederick and fluttered her eyelashes.

"Are you quite all right?" he asked. When she stopped

and nodded, he continued, "Now I have to leave and tell the housekeeper that we need the ballroom cleaned before eleven in the morning."

"Surely your staff keeps every inch of this place clean." Warwick said. "Certainly you can spend a little time with your charming fiancée."

"Yes, surely you could," Aphrodite echoed.

"I must make certain of the arrangement. I would not have it thought that Mother isn't a good housekeeper." He patted Aphrodite's hand. "I will see you tomorrow at the rehearsal, my dear Hermia."

"Helena," she corrected.

"Such passion overwhelms, my lady." Warwick leaned back in his chair to observe Aphrodite's reaction to her Frederick's departure.

"Not all of us are ruled by passion, my lord."

"Obviously not, but I would think you'd want better than a husband who is tied to his mother. You're too young to settle for that."

"Unfair, my lord. He is a devoted son, which means he will also be a devoted husband."

"Devotion is a poor substitution for passion."

"Oh, you are a romantic." Aphrodite scowled at him, then stopped as she felt those confounded wrinkles growing deeper. "I'd never have guessed that. However, given the choice of loving someone I could not trust or marrying a man I do trust, I would chose loyalty every time." She threw her head back for emphasis, a gesture she just realized she had inherited.

"Must you select one or the other? Certainly you don't have to give up affection for the sake of fidelity."

"Unfortunately, that has been my experience." She turned away from him, pretending to study a particularly hideous cherub that sat on the table next to her.

"I never realized you had an interest in poorly carved

marble." Warwick spoke over her shoulder, also studying the ugly little fellow.

She turned toward him to find his face next to hers, just a little higher. He looked down at her, his eyes serious. Then a look of warmth, almost of hunger, came over his face.

What was he thinking? His face looked almost as it had two years earlier when he'd lowered his mouth to hers. Aphrodite looked around to assure herself that there were people chatting in a room that to her had fallen silent.

If she hadn't seen that expression before, she might have thought he found her attractive, but she'd seen it and been fooled by it before.

"You are quite lovely," he said, his voice low and rough.

She had no will to break the intimacy of being held captive by his eyes, feeling his breath on her cheek and the warmth of his body so close to hers.

In the hush of the private moment, he put his hand on her shoulder and rested it there. She tilted her head up, as if waiting for his kiss. Then he touched her cheek with the back of his hand. Aphrodite stretched toward him, her mouth only inches from his, his gaze holding hers.

"I think I'll go to bed." Terpsi's voice rang out. "Ditie, Athena, are you coming?"

Aphrodite jerked, her head almost banging into Warwick's chin while he sprung away from her.

"Yes." Aphrodite leaped to her feet, gasping for air and fanning herself. "I think—" she paused, attempting to find the words to finish the sentence in her clouded brain. "I think," she began again, "that would be a good idea. Good night to all." She started toward the door, then stopped and touched her fingers to her cheek. She turned to look back at Warwick, but he was talking to Callum. She followed Terpsi's rapid stride from the room, almost unaware of what she was doing.

"Did you see that?" Terpsi growled when Aphrodite opened the door to her room. She pushed her way in front of Aphrodite, still grumbling.

Anger turned Terpsi into an Amazon. She stalked around the room, her hair crackling, her eyes sparkling. "Did you see what that man did? He was flirting, actually flirting, with that child, that infant!"

"What man, Terpsi? What child?" The rapid change of events confused Aphrodite. She struggled to grasp what had happened and what in the world Terpsi was babbling about.

She watched as Terpsi dramatically threw her arms open, but instead of being concerned about her sister's agitation, all Aphrodite could think was, *Why doesn't she go away and let me try to understand what just happened with Warwick?*

"Callum. He was flirting with the squire's daughter. She's a baby but *quite* the coquette."

With a sigh, Aphrodite turned her attention back to her sister. "You told me that there was nothing between you and Callum, that the romance was long over. Why are you so overset?"

Terpsi stopped her pacing. She looked sad and weary. Her usual brilliance and energy had abandoned her, and now she looked lost.

"I don't care about Callum any more." Terpsi's voice quivered. "I just don't want him to make a fool of himself, and I don't want that poor child to be taken in. Her heart could be broken and . . . and, well, who knows what?" Terpsi babbled.

"What are you going to do about it?" Aphrodite sat on the edge of the bed.

"Nothing." Terpsi's eyes showed bewilderment and pain. "I don't know. Don't you have any advice? What would *you* do?"

"It is your life, Terpsi. You must decide."

"Oh." Terpsi titled her head to consider that. "I see." Then she sat on the other side of the bed. "I'm just so confused about this, Ditie. You've always listened and had such good suggestions."

"You're grown up now, Terpsi. This is your life. You're going to have to make up your mind. You didn't tell me what happened when you and Callum stopped seeing each other." She held up a hand when Terpsi would have spoken. "And I think that was correct. You took care of that situation, and you can take care of this one."

"Oh?" Terpsi stood and started toward the door. "I will think about it." With a hint of the Terpsi that Aphrodite knew so well, she swirled and demanded, "But you will help me if I need you?"

"Of course, but right now, I want to go to bed. I have some things to consider."

"That's right. You must have a great deal to think about with your wedding to Mr. Horne to plan." Terpsi stalked from the room.

"Frederick," Aphrodite said aloud. Oh, my, she'd forgotten all about Frederick, forgotten that she was to marry him someday. Warwick's touch had chased everything else from her mind.

She had more to consider than she'd thought.

Aphrodite sat on the window seat and stared at the moon. She didn't love Frederick. She'd never deceived herself that she did, or that he loved her, but they suited. They would be comfortable together.

How good a wife would she be if she were irresistibly attracted to another man? Certainly not the wife Frederick or any man needed.

And yet, Warwick had broken her heart once. What was she thinking, to be bewitched by him again? It was more than foolish. It was idiotic. Reprehensible. Absurd.

But it felt so wonderful to be touched by him.

My goodness, she sounded like her sisters. She'd told them they were wantons, and here she was, dreaming about one man in the most inappropriate way while engaged to another. But she couldn't forget his caress or her unexpected response.

Frederick had never made her want to forget propriety, to throw herself into his arms, to run her fingers through his thick hair.

Stop! she told herself. And with the will forged by years of attempting to influence her brothers and sisters, she forced her thoughts away from Warwick and to the life she would share with Frederick. Safe and comfortable and dull.

She was, after all, the mature, dependable member of the family. She made decisions and stayed with them. Enough of moonlight, she decided. With that, she got in bed and fell asleep as soon as she pulled up the covers.

Warwick, however, was not in such an easy state of mind. He observed the same moon in the same sky, but his thoughts were much less sanguine.

He cursed himself for his foolishness, both now and in the past. How had he allowed himself to be attracted to her again? *Still.* Why hadn't he realized he'd never gotten over the chit, that he still remembered that one kiss. He wished he could have done it again, both in the garden two years ago and tonight in the drawing room, surrounded by his family and the man she would marry.

Devil a bit! He paced from one side of the room to the other, his hand ruining his hairstyle.

This was not a flirtation and never had been. From the time he'd stolen that kiss, he'd been done for. He hadn't admitted it, but it had happened. He'd been like a fish on a hook, dead for all practical purposes but still struggling.

What had begun as a game had changed, long ago. He was a perfect block, such a sapskull he hadn't seen it com-

ing and had walked straight into love without even notic-
ing. He'd come to Windwillow to woo and win Aphrodite.
He simply had not realized it until right now.

Well, there was nothing for it. He couldn't very well take
Aphrodite away from his own cousin, not even if he
thought it was best for her. He was a gentleman, and gentlemen didn't seduce innocent young women or steal fian-
cées from their cousins.

But when she'd looked up at him, he'd been enchanted.
This was the Aphrodite Herrington he'd always thought she
could be. Lovely. Delightful. The smile had enthralled him.
It was all over for him. He had finally fallen in love: with
the most ineligible of women.

She cared for him, too. If she were not so transparent,
he could pretend this feeling was only on his side, but it
wasn't. She had looked at him with love, an expression he
wagered Frederick would never see.

No, there was nothing for it. Tomorrow he would have
to act as if tonight had never happened. As if they hadn't
shared a moment alone in that crowd. As if they hadn't
fallen in love at that instant.

And, even more absurd, he'd fallen in love with a woman
he wasn't sure really existed outside of his imagination,
that he'd glimpsed only in one smile and tasted in a long-
ago kiss.

And she was engaged to his cousin.

No use going to bed. He poured himself a brandy from
the decanter Frederick kept in the rooms of male guests
and sat down. It would be a long time before he felt like
sleeping.

Chapter Eight

"'Now, fair Hippolyta, our nuptial hour draws on apace.' No, no, I don't believe that's regal enough." James intoned the part of Theseus, his chest lifted high. Aphrodite and James' wife Susannah sorted fabric for costumes while Athena studied her reflection in the windows along the north wall of the ballroom. At the other end of the ballroom, workmen had begun to construct a small stage.

"You sound wonderful, James. Very lordly." Aphrodite chose a length of pale pink muslin from a pile of fabric and held it under Athena's chin. "I think there is enough here for your costume, Athena, and the color is lovely on you."

"Oh, Ditie, isn't this exciting! I get to stand before hundreds of people and look beautiful."

"Probably not hundreds, Athena." Terpsi's voice and footsteps echoed in the cavernous room as she approached the group. "Perhaps twenty neighbors and family members."

"But I will still get to look beautiful, won't I?"

93

"Of course you will." Frederick's voice came from behind the stack of fabric he carried into the ballroom.

"Tell me, Mr. Horne. Which color looks better on me? The pink?" Athena held it in front of her. "Or the blue?"

"Lady Athena, there is no difference." Frederick dropped the fabric on Aphrodite's feet. "Both enhance your loveliness."

"Prettily said, Frederick." Aphrodite was startled at his eloquence.

"It is not difficult to praise the fair Herrington sisters," Frederick said as the rest of the cast entered the room.

"Do I need a play book?" Gwendolyn asked Terpsi, giggling as she held onto Callum's arm. "I know I have a little part. Perhaps I could share Mr. McReynold's." She looked up at him, eyes filled with adoration.

"I have enough for everyone." Terpsi spoke in icy tones. "No one need share." She passed the booklets to the assembled cast. "What is good about this play is that many scenes are between a few of the cast members, so we do not have to often practice together."

"Oh, Mr. McReynolds, do you have many scenes with the Queen of the fairies?" Gwendolyn asked.

"Fortunately, very few. Just a line here and there. Most of my scenes are with Puck." Mr. McReynolds turned to look at the young Italian noble, then frowned.

Wonderful, Aphrodite thought as she noticed Callum's scrutiny of Aski. Callum knows there's something havey-cavey going on. But certainly Aski had grown and changed since he'd known Callum. Unfortunately, today he had not worn his Italian disguise. He wore a nicely tailored brown coat with a beautifully embroidered waistcoat. Gone were the extravagant ribbons and bangles; only one thin band subdued his riotous curls.

By one o'clock, the actors had read all of Terpsi's adaptation of the drama and divided into sections. Aphrodite,

Frederick, Athena, and Warwick strolled to a lovely rose garden and began to practice.

After fifteen minutes, Aphrodite thought Warwick would strangle Athena. She could not pronounce Lysander, the name of her beloved, and the thought of plucking a crawling serpent from her breast, even an imaginary one, overset her. When she misread four out of five words, Warwick tossed down the play booklet in frustration.

"Ditie," Athena said, her eyes huge, begging her sister and Frederick to protect her. "Make him stop being mean to me."

"It won't do, you know," Aphrodite told him. "Getting angry with her will not resolve anything. If you are patient, Athena will do much better."

"She's like a fawn," Frederick added, glancing over his shoulder at Athena. "Timid and shy. If you alarm her, she'll quiver and run." He put his script down, went to Athena, and took her hands in his. "It will be fine, dear future sister-in-law. We will all work together."

"Thank you, Frederick. You are so kind." Color returned to Athena's cheeks as she looked worshipfully at him.

"Perhaps we should finish the scene," Warwick suggested. "I will make every effort to be more patient with the fair Hermia if she will attempt to read what is written."

"Of course she will." Frederick moved away from Athena toward Aphrodite. "And I will be happy to help her study her lines so she will feel more confident."

"I hope you will help her *learn* her lines," Warwick said.

"Learn my lines? I have to memorize all these words?" Tears gathered in Athena's eyes. "Ditie, I have to *memorize* everything? Can I not read from my play book?"

"Don't worry, Athena. We can discuss this later," Aphrodite promised. "Let's start at the beginning of the scene."

Since this didn't require Athena to do or say anything, she happily sat down to watch.

* * *

Later that day, as Warwick waited for his cousin in the hall outside the ballroom, he saw Frederick bowing to Athena and smiling into her enchanting blue eyes.

"If I may?" Warwick said when Frederick looked back over his shoulder at Athena. "As my father's representative, I would like to discuss a family matter with you."

"Certainly, cousin. Shall we go to my study?"

Warwick followed Frederick to a room across from Mrs. Horne's parlor. Warwick could not help but admire the masculine chamber as he settled himself in a comfortable chair upholstered in dark green.

"What is it, Thomas?" Frederick asked.

Warwick had not yet decided how to approach the subject. Indeed, even as the representative of his family, he probably didn't have any right to bring the matter up, but he must. It was the curse of caring, a curse which had never burdened him before. "I am concerned at how little time you spend with your future wife."

Frederick lifted an eyebrow at Warwick's comment. "What do you mean? She has come to this house party as the honored guest. What time I do not spend with my mother, I spend with Aphrodite."

"That's what I mean. Although I know how much you love your mother, perhaps you could spare a few moments for Lady Aphrodite? In the evening, you leave her with the other guests, without an escort."

"Certainly Aphrodite doesn't need an escort at a family house party. Her sisters are here, our family also."

"Yes, but she is to become your wife. You display little of the tender care and concern expected in a husband. Most of your time is spent with your mother." Warwick then added, as an afterthought, "or Lady Athena."

Frederick had leaned back in his chair but threw himself forward at the final words. His eyes sought Warwick's.

"What do you mean? You don't believe I nourish a *tendre* for the child, do you?"

Good heavens, Warwick thought. What had he uncovered? His cousin's reaction to the mention of Athena was surprising. "I mean only that you should spend some time with your betrothed."

"I do not understand your interest in this, Warwick, or your inferences about Lady Athena. She is a charming young lady who will be an nice addition to our family. I think of her as a sister already."

"It is a family matter, Frederick. If you dishonor your future bride, you dishonor the family."

"Quite right." Frederick cleared his throat. "I will certainly consider what you have said."

Warwick left the room and shrugged. There was nothing more he could do. He had put himself out far more than he had for anyone else, but had as little to show for it as if he had done nothing. This reminded him why he so seldom became involved in the problems of others.

However, that evening, Warwick noted that Frederick did not leave the parlor with his mother. Instead, he spent the evening in conversation with Aphrodite.

"I'm glad to see that," Susannah commented to her husband and brother as they discussed the progress of the play.

"See what?" James asked.

"That Frederick is spending more time with Aphrodite. I thought he neglected her terribly."

"I talked to him about that this afternoon." Warwick followed his sister's glance to where Frederick and Aphrodite engaged in a quiet conversation after his mother's departure.

"What? You did?" Susannah asked with surprise. "You actually discussed this with Frederick? When did you start taking an interest in other people?"

"Coming a little strong, dear sister. A family matter."

"True, true. A family matter," James agreed. "A man has to take care of family matters, my dear."

"Yes." Susannah studied Warwick. "It's just highly unusual for my brother to notice the concerns of others, even when it is a family matter."

"Speaking of unusual," Warwick looked around the room and chose another subject. "What do you know about Geoffrey's friend Luigi?"

"Oh, Thomas, he certainly has not fooled you, has he?"

"What do you mean?"

"It is obvious he's running a prank. If the young man's Italian, I'm Princess Charlotte. It's just the sort of thing you would have done in school."

"You don't mind that your son is taking part in whatever this is?" Warwick watched the young man flirt with the squire's youngest.

"Of course not. It's the sort of wheedle a young man cuts. Let's just enjoy it and see what happens. It's also clear that he is a well-born young man. At Cambridge, there's not much chance of Geoffrey meeting riffraff."

"You're right. Of no concern, but I wonder. Have you ever met the Herrington's son Aski? I believe he's also at the university."

Chapter Nine

Not for her the coy braids and ringlets other women chose, Terpsi thought as she studied herself in the mirror. Her hair curled over her shoulders. She shook her head to toss her shining tresses back so they would not detract from the snowy perfection of her skin.

Neither did she care about the approbation of society regarding what a proper young lady should wear. She was not proper. A voice whispered that she was no longer young either, but she ignored it. She was *not* proper, had never wanted to be proper, and hoped never to be proper.

But, perhaps, this dress went a little beyond the pale. Its neckline probably revealed a great deal more of Terpsi than was seemly, especially in the morning.

What difference does the clock make? she thought with another toss of her curls. If a dress were acceptable at a ball, why would it not be acceptable at any time?

Besides, only prigs could object. Highty-tighty people like Callum McReynolds, who constantly lectured her about her clothing and behavior, who condemned her with his eyes. Why should she care about people like that when she looked perfectly lovely? Perfectly and scandalously lovely.

People like Callum McReynolds needed to discover she cared not a whit about his opinions or censure.

A few years ago, she had wanted to win his approval. And what happened when she did that? During a perfectly delightful conversation, he'd put a shawl around her shoulders. She'd appreciated that on the cold evening. But then he'd arranged it so it covered her chest completely. With a toss of her head, she'd turned to flirt with another man. When she turned back, Callum was gone and she hadn't seen him again until now.

She didn't care a jot. She wasn't going to throw her hat at a man. Lady Terpsichore Herrington didn't need to. Men flocked to her when she spoke in her low voice or when she smiled at them in a certain way.

No one needed a prim and proper Scot to tell her how to behave. Never again would she allow him to cut up her peace and leave her sobbing. With that, she thrust out her chest, tossed her head, and left the room.

But only an hour later, she discovered that the Scot could still cut up her peace.

"Don't look at me that way," Terpsi whispered to Callum, who stared at her disapprovingly. She attempted to concentrate on Aski as Puck and Elsie as a fairy while they read their parts, but the man made it impossible.

"If you didn't dress as you do, Lady Terpsichore, you would not be bothered with men looking at you in a manner that you find distasteful." Callum's expression was grim and disapproving.

"I most certainly do not dress this way to attract men," Terpsi said, her voice getting louder.

"Then what other reason do you have?" Callum bellowed.

"Comfort!" she shouted.

"Comfort?" he yelled back at her. "I would think it would be most uncomfortable to be constantly putting one's dress back on one's shoulders or pulling it up to cover one's chest. And I would think you must be cold displaying so much of yourself. *That* cannot be comfortable."

"You self-righteous coxcomb, what right do you have to say that?"

"No right, thank goodness, but I am a friend of a man who is about to join your family, and your nakedness dishonors both families."

Then Terpsi looked over Callum's shoulder and realized that the cast had stopped reading their lines. From the other side of the room, the four lovers—Aphrodite, Athena, Warwick and Frederick—stared at the arguing couple. Susannah had stopped stitching costumes to watch them while Aski and Elsie watched from only a few feet away.

"It's nothing," Terpsi explained. "I'm sorry. We were just practicing our lines."

The cast looked down at their scripts as if trying to find where Shakespeare had written such words.

"Aski . . . I mean, Luigi, if you will start your lines again," Terpsi prompted.

"What's this mean, Terpsi?" Aski asked, showing her a line in his booklet. He forgot his accent and that, as Conti di Versati, he wouldn't know this woman well enough to use her name. "This line says, 'But they do square.' "

"It means they quarrel."

Aski looked at his book. "So Oberon and Titania quarrel? So much that the fairies all hide?" He began to laugh. "That's just like you and Callum. How interesting you two would be cast as sweethearts who fight all the time."

When Callum studied Aski again, the younger man said, "Oh, excusea me. I didna mean to be so forward."

"Who is that?" Callum demanded. "He can't be Italian.

Sounds Irish. Not Scotch, but something other than Italian."
He turned to glare at Terpsi. "How does he know you and
I fought a lot? Why does he call you by your first name?
Are you keeping company with him? Isn't he a little young,
even for you?"

"Yes, he's too young, *even for me*." Terpsi glowered
back at him. "All society knows you and I fought. Perhaps
he heard about it from his parents. Now, let us return to
the play."

Twenty minutes later, the cast left for their luncheon, but
not before Aski caught Aphrodite's eye.

"By the lake," he mouthed. "Now."

Aphrodite nodded, then turned to discover that Warwick
stood behind her. "May I escort you to the yellow salon
where I believe the food is laid out?"

"No, thank you." Oh, she was such a bad liar. What
excuse could she give? "My costume." She grabbed up a
piece of muslin. "Susannah asked me to try this on. To see
if it fit."

Warwick took the length of fabric from her hands. "Certainly this can't be your gown. I don't believe Susannah
has taken a stitch in it."

"Yes, it is," she insisted as she took the length of muslin
from him. "I will see you this afternoon." She caught herself before she started to babble nervously, then dashed for
the front hall and climbed the stairs, as if she were going
to her chambers. When she saw the party disappear toward
the dining area, she tossed the fabric behind a column, scur-
ried down the stairs and out the front door, racing down
the path to the lake.

"What is the reason for this tryst?" Aphrodite glared at
her brother as she gasped for air.

"Can't a fellow want to talk to his sister?" Aski asked
with a smile of such charm that she knew he was planning
the impossible.

"About what?"

"Don't sound so suspicious, Ditie. I've decided it's time to go back to school. This was a lark for a while, but Geoffrey and I should go back. Could you find out if the magistrate is still looking for us?"

"How would I do that?"

"I don't know, Ditie. You usually work things out for us."

"Perhaps I should go to Cambridge?"

"That would be just the thing! Would you?"

"Of course, not, Aski. You got into this fix. It's up to you to decide how to get out of it."

"But, Ditie, you have always helped me."

"Yes, I have, but not this time, Aski. I warned you, and you didn't listen. I will do so no more." She pointed at the furrows between her brow. "Look, this is what helping and worrying about you has gotten me. I have wrinkles. I'm only twenty, and I have wrinkles!"

"But, Ditie, you always . . ."

"You're repeating yourself." She started toward the house.

Only a few minutes after Aphrodite had gone to meet Aski, Terpsi sat on the bench overlooking the lake. She looked at the words in her script but they seemed to mock her. " 'I have forsworn his company,' " she read and sighed. Yes, she had forsworn his company. Did even the Bard have to remind her of that? Titania and Oberon battled as did she and Callum.

" 'Ill met by moonlight, proud Titania.' " Terpsi heard a low voice and looked up to see Hugh Ridley approaching her bench.

"But 'tis barely noon, sir." She laughed up at him and tugged on the neckline of her dress.

"I am wondering about your friendship with Mr. Mc-

Reynolds. You have a previous acquaintance, I would guess." Hugh crossed the stone terrace and sat next to her.

"Yes, from years in the past. We do not get along."

"I would think such enmity does not come from friendship or indifference."

"That's correct. Mr. McReynolds courted me once, but that was when I was younger and less discerning."

"And you feel nothing for him now?"

"Nothing." She shifted to look toward the lake instead of at him. "Nothing at all."

"And that is why you are angry whenever you are in his company?" He turned on the bench and studied her profile.

"Why is it your concern?"

"Because I find you very lovely and would like to see you once we return to London, but if Mr. McReynolds . . ."

"It is likely that he will return to Scotland shortly. You may have noticed that he is not a fashionable man, as are you. He cares nothing for the city or fine clothing."

"And yet you allowed him to court you? Lady Terpsichore, please forgive me if I insult you, but I thought you loved society life."

"At the time, I decided that there was something better than living in London and was quite prepared to sacrifice, but such was not asked for. That was many years ago."

"Then you will not mind if I call on you? Perhaps you would go for a drive with me in the park?"

"Why would you want to?" Terpsi considered her conduct for the past few days. "I have behaved terribly and rudely."

"But with such fire and passion, Lady Terpsichore. You Herringtons live life so fully. I find it exciting just to be around you. The air positively hums."

"Then I would be delighted, Mr. Ridley." Terpsi smiled at him as a panting Aphrodite passed the bench on her way back to the house, followed a short time later by Aski. "I have finished studying my part. Would you take me in to the luncheon?"

"I would be delighted, Lady Terpsichore." He placed her hand on his arm and helped her over the uneven stones.

They had just stepped on the driveway when Terpsi saw Warwick emerge from the woods, his dark coat covered with leaves. She'd wager that his boots were scratched, too. She smiled. Warwick and her proper sister? What about Mr. Horne? She knew better than to think her sister would break an engagement, but this was not, after all, a real engagement yet.

When she noted Callum looking out the window of the yellow salon, Terpsi favoured Ridley with an enchanting smile and a burst of laughter.

That afternoon Aphrodite, Athena, Frederick and Warwick gathered around the same bench. They had enjoyed a lovely light repast, then Athena had napped in her room while the others read their lines to each other. When a rested Athena came toward the small group, Aphrodite couldn't help but think how lovely she was, with her enchanting smile and hair as pale as moonbeams.

Neither could Frederick take his eyes from the young woman. Warwick's gaze darted from Aphrodite to her sister, then to her fiancé and back to Aphrodite again.

"And your conclusion?" Aphrodite asked Warwick in a low voice when she noticed his observation.

"I will apprise you of it at the proper time," he whispered before greeting his acting partner. "Good afternoon, Lady Athena. You look refreshed. Are you ready to practice?"

"Susannah said that she was going into the village to look for some lace, Ditie. I would so love to go." Athena looked beseechingly at her sister.

"I know you would, dear, but Susannah has such a small part. She has additional time. And the lace is for the costumes she is spending so much time making. Let us read our lines for an hour or so, then, perhaps Frederick would take us for a ride in his new phaeton."

"Certainly, my lady." Frederick nodded to Athena.

"I want to go now." Athena's eyes narrowed and her lips formed a puckered circle.

Aphrodite blanched. Athena had worked herself into a temper and she hated for anyone to witness it. The child didn't realize how disagreeable it made her look. "Why don't we read through this scene once, then we'll take a walk together and practice."

"No, no, *no!*" Athena threw her book on the ground.

"Lady Athena, you must still be exhausted from the long morning and not quite awake from your rest." Frederick placed her hand on his arm and led her to the bench. "Let us sit here for a while and look at the scenery. Have you ever seen a more pleasant prospect?" He patted her hand and lowered her onto the seat like a fragile doll. "Now, isn't this delightful?"

Athena stared up into Frederick's eyes and sighed. "Oh, so lovely. You see, I've been worried. I know Warwick will expect me to memorize my lines, and I *cannot* do that. You know that, Ditie," she spoke to her sister over her shoulder, then turned back to face Frederick. "She knows I cannot memorize things."

"Yes, dear. Perhaps we could shorten some speeches."

"They are shortened, Aphrodite," Warwick reminded her. "Were they any shorter, she would be silent on the stage, merely moving back and forth."

"And looking beautiful," Frederick added.

"Oh, yes!" Athena clapped her hands. "That's exactly what I want."

"I am to speak my lines to a lovely statue?" Warwick asked.

"See, I knew he'd be angry." Athena's lip quivered. "I

cannot work with him," she said to Frederick, tears again gathered in the azure depths of her eyes. "Please, would you change parts with him? Would you be Lysander?"

"I don't know." He looked to Aphrodite for guidance.

"Oh, please." Athena turned to her sister. "Please say that will be all right, Ditie. I am so afraid of Warwick."

"If you want your sister to live, you will accept the exchange," Warwick muttered in Aphrodite's ear.

"Yes, that will be fine," Aphrodite agreed. "Then shall I be Hermia?"

"No, no, Ditie. I do know a few of her words and I will read the rest."

"I'm sure that will be fine, Lady Athena." Frederick patted her hand again. "We will tell Lady Terpsichore in the morning."

"Won't she be pleased," Warwick added.

"Will she mind?" Athena's eyes began to tear again.

"Not at all, darling." Aphrodite glared at Warwick. "I will talk to her and explain everything. I know she will understand if *other people* will keep their mouths closed and their opinions to themselves."

"Of course, Aphrodite." Warwick took her hand and placed it on his arm. "Shall we take a walk and discuss our parts while Frederick and Athena read theirs together? I believe tea is being served on the lawn."

They moved away from the bench to stroll around the maze, through a statuary garden, then toward the front drive where Puck and Oberon read together. As they passed them, Warwick said, "During rehearsals, I've noticed the conti's accent disappears when he reads his part. In fact, there are times he sounds like a young man from Cambridge. Why do you suppose that is?"

Aphrodite glanced at him. He was laughing at her, but she had to say something. "I believe he studied Shakespeare with a British tutor."

"Oh, indeed." He considered that for a moment. "And he is so impressionable that he picked up the tutor's accent?" He helped Aphrodite over a rough section of the path.

"Yes, I believe so." She spoke, she hoped, with authority.

"If that is true, why does he have such a strong and odd Italian accent at all other times?"

"His region of Italy . . ."

"Oh, yes, his region of Italy. To be sure." He looked at her with a smile. "I wish you believed that I stand your friend, that you can call on me if the scamp is causing you problems."

He looked down at her, a soft, gentle light in his eyes, as if he really did want to help her. Oh, how she wished she could share some of the burden of her family with him. But before she could utter another word, Frederick approached and took Aphrodite's arm.

"There you are, Aphrodite." Frederick appeared beside her and nodded at Thomas. "I am glad you found the tea table. May I get you a cup?" He held out his arm and she put her hand on it.

Frederick led her away from Warwick and toward the refreshment table where a servant handed her a cup of tea.

Her eyes shifted across the lawn to where Athena stood with Fothergill, shyly gazing up at him.

"Your younger sister is nearly as enchanting as you are. Please tell me, is anyone courting Lady Athena?"

"No, not at the moment."

"I am sure she attracts a great deal of attention with the gentlemen," Frederick continued.

"Yes, she does." Aphrodite studied her fiancé, then her sister, and wondered. Then her glance moved around the guests until it returned to Warwick.

As if he felt her eyes, Warwick turned and watched her, a glance filled with emotion. What he felt, Aphrodite was not sure, but she could not breathe. It was the same look she had seen her father give her mother. And she knew she was returning that look, with the same invitation her mother gave her father.

For a moment, she felt as if they were alone on a beautiful green island, just the two of them, surrounded by a broad blue sky and warmed by soft, lavender-scented breezes.

Then Frederick made another comment about something, and she wrenched her gaze away from Warwick. Of course she was not alone. She shared a bench with her fiancé, but when she turned to speak to him, she recognized that he was more than a little dull.

In that same instant, she realized that he was paying a great deal of attention to her little sister.

Chapter Ten

At the rehearsal late that afternoon, Aphrodite studied the group gathered in the ballroom. Only Warwick still looked alive and awake, holding pins as the squire's wife fitted Athena's drape.

"I hereby declare that tomorrow will be a holiday for all the fairies and denizens of ancient Greece," Aphrodite announced. "No more thoughts of *A Midsummer Night's Dream*. Everyone sleep late in the morning. Frederick," she turned toward her almost-fiancé, who was helping Athena read her lines. "Can your cook put together a picnic by the lake for tomorrow afternoon?"

"I'm sure that will be no trouble."

"Then tomorrow, everyone, go to town or take walks until late afternoon. After dinner, let's gather for just a short time to fit the costumes."

"Ditie, the play is only four days away. This leaves us so little time." Terpsi frowned.

"I know, dear, but everyone is so tired. We'll all come back ready to work again tomorrow."

Unwillingly, Terpsi agreed and the cast scattered.

As had been suggested, all slept late and ate breakfast in their rooms. A note came on Aphrodite's tray that Mrs. Horne was indisposed and Frederick would be caring for his mother all day. Athena arrived shortly after.

"Oh, Ditie, I'm so excited that we're not reading that play again," Athena said as she sat on the bed. "Although," Athena paused to chew her lip. "Although it has not all been terrible. I have to say Mr. Horne isn't as boring as I thought he was."

"Oh?"

"I mean, I told you I thought he was an old stick. Mayhap that's not all bad. Warwick frightens me. Mr. Horne is much more . . . oh, I don't know. Comfortable."

Aphrodite said, "What do you mean, Athena?"

"Well, he's not really dull. He's soothing and patient." Athena bounced on the bed. "I've learned a line or two with his help." Then she stood and flounced toward the mirror and studied her reflection, smoothing her dress and patting her hair.

"What are you planning to do today?" Aphrodite asked.

"I may go with Susannah and her daughters to the village."

With that, Athena danced toward the door and into the hallway.

Aphrodite re-read Frederick's note as she strolled across the entrance hall. It seemed Mrs. Horne had become ill during the night.

"Something she ate. Possibly a cow or a chicken." Warwick's voice intruded into her thoughts.

Aphrodite turned. He stood much closer than she expected. When she took a step back, away from the lure of his charm, he smiled. He most certainly knew the effect he had on women. She must be ridiculously easy for such a man to read.

"I don't know why she is ill. Frederick is staying with

her, to read to her and encourage her to eat something. I believe he said something about calves' foot jelly," she responded.

"A particular favorite of Aunt Matilda's, but what isn't?"

"Which I have heard is a wonderful restorative," she finished, ignoring Warwick's interruption.

"If you think Aunt Matilda needs a restorative, you don't know her well. She's not sick, just tired of sharing her son."

He took a step toward her, but Aphrodite held her ground. "What do you plan to do today?" he asked.

"I haven't decided. Perhaps I'll write my parents and some of my brothers and sisters."

"Even allowing for the size of your family, fair Patience, that cannot take more than an hour or two of your time."

"I wish you would not call me that. It's a foolish name and does not fit me at all." She looked around and realized how alone they were. The privacy of the isolated front of the house suddenly became very intimate. Almost in a panic, she bolted for the morning room where she knew there would be company.

She waited in the door for almost a minute, but when he didn't appear in the hallway, she entered the morning room and joined the ladies stitching costumes.

That afternoon, most of the actors had assembled to look at their costumes or help others with theirs. A recovered Mrs. Horne sat next to her son and surveyed the scene before her.

"Oh, I'm so glad to see you." Susannah rushed toward Aphrodite before Mrs. Horne could tap her cane and demand Aphrodite attend her. Susannah held a length of light muslin in her hands. "I need to see you in your costume. It's almost finished. You're wearing the white robe with blue trim. Athena's is white with pink trim. It's very loose. I'll just drape it over your dress." Susannah dropped the gown over Aphrodite's head and pulled it into place.

"Now, let me put the sash around you." She draped a length of blue cord behind Aphrodite's neck, crossed it over her chest, then tied it behind her back. "I think I remember old pictures that show Greek maidens dressed like this."

"It feels comfortable." With the sudden hush in the room, Aphrodite looked up to see that everyone was staring at her.

"I didn't realize . . . ," Susannah began, her eyes directed toward Aphrodite's bosom.

"It seems to emphasize my chest," Aphrodite whispered.

"I noticed that," Susannah replied in a low voice. "Perhaps I could loosen the trim or tie it another way."

"Behold!" Mrs. Horne's voice echoed through the small room. "Your chosen could be mother to a nation." She turned toward Frederick who was attempting to swallow and speak at the same time.

Aphrodite looked around, amazed at what Mrs. Horne had said.

Her first reaction was to cover her chest with her arms but she thought that would draw even more attention. She could see the shock on the faces of all the guests, even Warwick's.

"Mother," Frederick said when he could finally speak. "I think such a comment embarrasses Lady Aphrodite.

Aphrodite began to shake. She put her head in her hands and turned away from the group, attempting to get out the door before emotion overwhelmed her. She had almost escaped from the ballroom when Warwick reached her. He put his arm around her and guided her out into the hallway. He made ineffectual masculine attempts to comfort her by pulling her against his broad chest, then patting her on the shoulder and murmuring, "There, there."

"It's all right." Aphrodite gasped as she tried to take another breath before going off in a paroxysm of laughter. "I'm fine," she managed to choke out between chortles.

"You're not crying," Warwick said, stunned. "You're laughing."

"Yes, I am." She looked up at him as a gurgle escaped her throat. "Please forgive me. I'm afraid I've become irreverent and am completely unrepentant. Excuse me. I need to get farther away from the doorway so no one will hear me." She ran off to a corridor leading away from the ballroom where she leaned against the wall and allowed herself to burst out in gales of laughter.

Warwick followed her and looked at her with an expression she could not decipher. Amazement was part of it, but there was something more, a warmth she couldn't understand.

"I must confess, Mrs. Horne makes me realize I am more of a Herrington than I thought. What a surprise! At this moment, I really enjoy it." She wiped the tears from her eyes with the corner of her costume.

"You are enchanting," he murmured. "Completely charming. I don't believe Frederick realizes what a fortunate man he is." He picked up her hands and held them between his.

"Oh, la," Aphrodite said, then laughed again. "Oh, my, I can't believe I said that," as she pulled one of her hands away and pressed it against her warm cheeks. "I never say that. I sound like Athena."

"Aphrodite?" a male voice called down the hallway.

Oh, dear, she thought when she identified Frederick's voice. She pulled the other hand from Warwick's grasp and patted her unruly hair.

"I'm here," she called. With a quick glance at Warwick, she stepped away from him. "In this hallway."

"I'm sorry about what mother said." Frederick hurried toward her voice. "I have attempted to get her to hold her tongue, but she had an earthy upbringing, which shows in odd moments."

"It doesn't matter, Frederick." Aphrodite turned the corner and almost ran into him.

"But you must have been mortified. I'm sorry it took me this long to come after you. Mother—" He saw Warwick behind her and broke off. Through narrowed eyes, he looked from Warwick to Aphrodite, and finally back to Warwick.

"I am fine," Aphrodite assured him. "Warwick comforted me."

"Thomas?" Now Frederick's mouth dropped as he stared at Warwick. "*Thomas* comforted you?"

"Why, yes." Warwick raised his eyebrow. "You find that odd?"

"You've never comforted anyone in your life," Frederick began, but the chill of Warwick's expression stopped him. "I mean, how nice of you to take care of *my* fiancée." Then his eyes moved to Aphrodite and he noticed her pink cheeks for the first time. "Have you been crying, Aphrodite?" he asked. "Or are your cheeks still flushed from mortification?"

"Mortification," Warwick supplied.

"And you were comforting her?" Frederick murmured again.

"He was most comforting. I felt very . . . comforted." Aphrodite said.

"I don't know why you're always cutting up rough at me." Terpsi's shriek broke into the odd conversation among Frederick, Aphrodite, and Warwick.

Aphrodite looked up as Callum stomped from the morning room and into the hall, pursued by her sister.

"Why do you always criticize me?" Terpsi shouted at his back, but Callum kept going. She stopped after a dozen steps and all her vitality seemed to drain out.

" 'The course of true love never . . .' " Warwick quoted. But Aphrodite didn't hear the rest of his words as she rushed toward Terpsi. With a practiced movement, she took her sister's arm and led her up the stairs to her bedroom. Once there, she forced her sister to lie down and bathed her face in lavender water. When Terpsi was a little calmer, Aphrodite held her hand.

"Do you want to talk about what happened?" Aphrodite asked when Terpsi had stopped quivering.

"Oh, Ditie, I'm so miserable."

"You're in love with him. Still." Aphrodite pushed the hair back from her sister's forehead.

Terpsi buried her head in the pillow. "And I've made such a mull of it."

"What are you going to do?"

Terpsi sat up, knocking Aphrodite's hand away. "What am I going to do? Why should I do anything? I'm not the one who walked out on him without a word, not even 'goodbye,' not telling him what was wrong or what I wanted."

"Oh." After a pause, Aphrodite asked, "What happened?"

"Go away." Terpsi threw herself on the bed and closed her eyes. "I'm sorry, Ditie. I don't want to talk about this now."

After a few minutes, Aphrodite accepted the fact that Terpsi was not going to explain and left, although the sight of tears squeezing under her sister's eyelashes broke her heart. But Terpsi was old enough to solve her own problems. Aphrodite closed the door softly behind her.

"Frederick," Athena said. "While Ditie is busy with our sister, would you please rehearse one of our scenes with me?"

But Frederick turned and continued to look up the staircase, concern apparent in his posture.

"Please, Frederick? Ditie is so good at taking care of Terpsi, and we have so little time to work together before the performance." She placed her tiny hand on Frederick's sleeve.

When he looked down at her, she pleaded, "Please? It is so hard for me to learn lines." She fluttered her eyelashes at him, then watched with dismay as his eyes took on the unfocused look she often produced in a man. Oh, dear, she reminded herself, this was *Ditie's* fiancé and he most definitely should not be gazing at her in that way. She must not flirt with Ditie's fiancé, although she wasn't sure how *not* to flirt with a man.

She led him to the overlook, reminding herself not to flirt. "I brought two booklets with me. Perhaps if we started on Act One, Scene One?"

Athena sat, then smiled up at Frederick.

"Yes, yes." He blinked rapidly, as men often did when she smiled, then took one of the booklets and opened it. "Ah, here we are. 'How now, my love! why is your cheek so pale? How chance the roses there do fade so fast?' "

"I think the next words are so silly. 'Belike for lack of rain, which I could well beteem them from the tempest of my eyes.' I *cannot* remember the words I do not know. Could I not say, 'I have been crying a lot lately'?"

"It doesn't quite preserve the feel of Shakespeare. Perhaps I could think of a way to change the line so you would feel better about saying it. Let us continue."

"Oh, it is so wonderful to practice with you," Athena said. "Warwick scares me, but you are so understanding."

"Thank you."

"No, I must thank you for spending time with me." She lowered her eyes. "You are such a nice man. You make me feel safe."

Unable to speak, he took her hand in his. He sat for a full minute holding her hand before he seemed to wake up and realize where he was. He dropped her hand and leaped from the bench.

"If you will excuse me, Lady Athena. I need to speak with your sister—my fiancée, your sister—and see how my mother is." He turned and almost ran toward the house.

Oh, dear, Athena thought. She must not allow him to hold her hand or sit with her and gaze on her beauty.

But he did make her feel so safe.

Chapter Eleven

Aphrodite dropped the curtain over the window. Dark clouds that threatened rain hid the early morning light.

She hadn't slept well. Terpsi's shouts had echoed in her mind, followed by pictures of Aski in his foolish disguise. Thank goodness he hadn't caused many problems lately, but it was absurd to trust any of her siblings to behave themselves for any reasonable length of time.

Additionally, she'd worried because Frederick spent all his time with his mother and ignored her, his fiancée-to-be. Would he always be his mother's son, not her husband? It didn't bode well for a marriage.

Mama and Papa loved being together. She'd always believed she and her husband would enjoy each other as they did. Well, perhaps not exactly as her parents did, but she had believed they would like to be together, that they would not allow anyone to interfere with spending time in each other's company.

She was blue-deviled. Could anything else go wrong? Please, dear Lord, nothing else. If anything more were to happen, she would just wash her hands of her family and Windwillow and run back to London.

How wonderful it would be if there were a person with whom she could share the burden of her family and the responsibility that went with being the only sensible one. Oh, she wished there would be another person who would help her and love her and comfort her, as Warwick had for a moment. She left the house and stamped to the small clearing overlooking the lake, taking deep breaths of the humid air. The clouds parted, and a ray of sunshine fell on the white marble summer house below her.

After a moment, Aphrodite heard a noise and opened her eyes. Warwick stood before her. She closed her eyes again.

"Don't try to ignore me, fair Patience."

"I am not patient," she snapped. "I wish you would stop using that absurd nickname. I am the most impatient person I know." Her voice had risen to an ear-splitting level. "Please go away and leave me alone or I shall be even ruder to you."

"You have much more patience than do I. If your brothers and sisters were mine, I would have murdered the lot of them years ago." When her eyes shot open and a militant sparkle appeared within them, he hastened to say, "Don't cut up rough with me. I know you love them, but they are a rare handful, and you know that. You've spent your entire life getting them out of one scrape after another. Perhaps it's time to quit." He sat on the wall and scrutinized her.

Although she had come to the same conclusion herself, she glared at him.

"What is causing your unhappiness?" He took her hands with one of his and massaged her brow with the other.

"It's nothing," she snapped and stepped away from him so his hands fell in his lap. "Just a future *belle-mère* who would frighten Wellington, a fiancé who spends all his time with her, a brother who commits the greatest of follies, and a man who places wagers about my character in the books at White's."

She hadn't meant to say that last. It had tumbled out with her other grievances.

"Shall we discuss those issues one at a time?" Warwick grasped both her hands in his. "Would you believe me if I told you that I didn't place that wager?" He waited. When she didn't reply, he continued. "I went there with several friends who had seen us dance together the previous evening."

Aphrodite looked over his shoulder to study the lake below her. She could feel his eyes searching her face. Then he turned her hand over and began to rub her palm.

"They seemed to believe there was something between us."

Aphrodite stared at him and again pulled her hand from his. "What do you mean? There has never . . . well, there may have been once, for a short while two years ago, but it was ephemeral. No one else knew about it."

"My friends thought they saw an attraction between us that evening."

"Absurd." Aphrodite walked to the other end of the balustrade. "Passion? I don't feel . . . do you? Between us?"

"You must have felt it." He got to his feet to stand next to her. "I know you did. I am not the only one to have noticed it. All my friends did. Certainly you must have felt something."

"A few years ago, yes, I felt an attraction for you, but it came to naught." She moved away from him.

"Yes, it came to naught. Neither of us was ready for that. You were too young, and I was too wild, unable to recognize love. But I never forgot that kiss." He stopped and smiled when he saw her look of disbelief. "I was not ready at that time to care for just one woman. That does not mean that nothing happened."

"The next night, I saw you kiss Leticia." She turned toward him, her eyes flashing and her breast heaving with anger, but when she saw the admiration in his eyes, she stepped away from him. "No, that was not the time and neither is this. Remember, I am engaged to your cousin."

"Only if Aunt Matilda agrees," he reminded her. "But I must know. Do you believe that I didn't make the wager? That it was made in my name? I would never do anything to hurt your reputation."

"Yes, I believe you." She attempted to push past him but he blocked her way.

"Well, if we have cleared that up, suppose you tell me about this brother who commits the greatest of follies and probably expects you to clean up after him."

"It is nothing. I need to return to the house."

Aphrodite moved past him when he stepped aside but stopped when he spoke again.

"I know that the conte or the conti, whichever, is really your brother Asklepios. Do you want to tell me more? I wish you would believe that I stand as your friend and would like to help you."

"You know? How?" She turned and stared at him.

"It was not difficult. He obviously wasn't Italian, and Susannah says Geoffrey has spoken about your brother. You said he was a scamp. He looks like a Herrington; he acts like one."

"Oh." Aphrodite dropped onto the bench, then looked up at him. "Does everyone know?"

"Probably. They are just pretending not to. Susannah said she thought it was a wonderful prank." He sat next to her. "Do you want to tell me about it? Or do you prefer to carry the burden alone?"

"No, it would be very nice to talk about it with someone who has an ounce of understanding." She looked up at him, stricken. "Oh, I didn't mean that to insult you. Terpsi believes Aski's disguise is a marvelous antic, and Athena hasn't even noticed he's here. They are no help at all."

"Well, why don't you tell me?" Warwick held up his hand. "I promise I will not tell another person."

The story of Aski and Geoffrey's adventure with the recently deceased dog caused Warwick's lips to quiver. By the time she had finished the story, both were chuckling.

"Oh, it is so foolish, I know, but Aski is right. If our father ever finds out about this, Aski will be in great trouble."

"I would have thought that Aski was used to being in great trouble."

"Yes, he is, but Papa is different. He can make you feel like such a failure. We would rather be harshly punished than have to face him."

"Wouldn't Aski foresee the consequences of his actions? Why would he pull this prank if he didn't want to have to face his father?"

"Certainly you know my family by now, Thomas. Most Herringtons do not foresee the consequences of their actions, an unfortunate family trait which some find quite charming."

"But which has caused his loving sister grief." said Thomas.

"Oh, no!" Aphrodite turned toward him, eyes wide in amazement. "Concern, but not grief. My family entertains me as much as it confounds me."

"And yet you spend so much time rescuing them."

"In the past, I have, but no longer. I have decided it is quite up to them to get out of their scrapes without me."

"A commendable resolution, fair Patience, but breaking the habit of years . . ."

"May be difficult," Aphrodite agreed. "But it is necessary. After all, when I am married—" she could not look into his eyes as she said this, and her voice faltered. "When

I am married, I will not be able to rescue them, I will have to look after my . . ." Again the words stuck in her throat. "My children, not my siblings."

"My bitch at Crusader's Cross just threw a litter," Warwick said. "I think a magistrate might look kindly upon receiving a pup from the future Earl of Wharton, don't you? After all, consequence should be good for something, perhaps to relieve part of the burden from one I can help."

"Would you? Would you really?" Then her delight turned to distress. "No, no, that isn't possible. I would be rescuing him again. Or, you would be."

"I am not rescuing *him*," Warwick said with such a gentle tone in his voice that Aphrodite turned to look into eyes filled with understanding and compassion. "I wish to help a most valiant and loving sister, to remove the frown and worry from her face."

"Oh!" Aphrodite's hands flew to the furrows between her eyebrows. "I had hoped no one had noticed."

"They are almost imperceptible." Warwick took her hands and held them. "You have cared for your family alone for far too long. Please let me help you."

"But why?"

"Because I would like to see you smile again, to watch you dance as you did at Almack's, as if without a care. I want to see you rested and calm so those tiny lines of worry will disappear."

"But why?"

Warwick studied her face for a moment. She could see the gentleness in his eyes turn to a glitter. What that meant, she didn't know, but she had a hard time catching her breath.

Idiot, she told herself. You have forgotten yourself with this man before. But she couldn't break the pull of his gaze or the desire she felt to move closer to him. And she was, after all, soon to be formally engaged to Warwick's cousin, she reminded herself.

"Aphrodite?"

Both she and Warwick turned to see Frederick walking toward them. Warwick dropped her hand and she moved away from him.

"What are you doing out here?" Frederick demanded. "I've been looking everywhere for you."

"Oh, Warwick and I were just discussing the weather."

Frederick studied the slate grey sky. "Windy and wet for a stroll, I would think."

Warwick spoke slowly and forcefully. "And yet, I was taking a walk when I discovered Lady Aphrodite here, enjoying the sunshine." The clouds floated across the sun again.

A sudden gust of wind tore Aphrodite's bonnet from her head and tossed it across the grass toward the driveway.

"Excuse me, I must finish my walk." Warwick nodded at them. "And I will capture your charming hat and return it to you."

Aphrodite placed her hand on the arm of her fiancé-to-be and nodded.

"What about breakfast?" Frederick asked her. "I waited to eat it with you. That is why I was searching for you. Mother is feeling much better."

"I am glad she has recovered. Perhaps I will ring for some chocolate and toast." She started up the stairs, then turned back to Frederick with a smile, "I am sorry I missed eating with you. Perhaps if you will let me know next time when you are available. I would like to spend time with my husband-to-be."

The words rang false to her ears.

Chapter Twelve

Warwick turned Aphrodite's bedraggled hat in his hands. The formerly stiff brim flopped in his hands and the pink flowers were speckled with dirt and grass.

He rubbed his thumb over the leaf and thought of the hat's owner, the beautiful woman who was also the most loyal and loving of people. Who was betrothed, nearly, to his cousin.

Lord, he was becoming maudlin. If this is what love did to a man, he wanted no part of it, but he feared it was too late for him to disown the emotion. He loved her whether she smiled up at him or she told him to leave her alone.

But, she was as good as engaged to Frederick and he hadn't come, as head of the family, to take his cousin's intended from him. At least, he had not recognized that when he rushed to Windwillow.

As a gentleman, he could not declare himself. She must know he was attracted, yet he could not tell her how much. It was probable, after the way he had flirted with her in the past, she'd never believe that he loved her. Devil it, he wanted to marry her.

126

The only woman he'd ever loved enough to wish to marry was engaged, almost, to his cousin. Could he live with the knowledge that another man would touch her, would father her children?

Well, if he couldn't declare himself, he'd do something to help her. A poor present, but the only one he could properly give to his love.

He'd already asked his coachman to ready the whiskey and would soon ask Taylor to go to Crusader's Cross to pick the puppy most likely to win a little girl's heart and soften her father's.

The house party had gathered in the parlor after dinner. Frederick had seated Aphrodite next to his sleeping mother and the two chatted pleasantly around Mrs. Horne's girth and over the thunder of her snores.

Close to the fireplace, Callum McReynolds sat with the squire's older daughter, but their conversation had lapsed. She giggled, and he glowered into the fire while Terpsi flirted with Hugh Ridley and Fothergill. When her neckline gaped, she put a hand on her chest or on her shoulder to haul it back into place.

"I heard you sent to Crusader's Cross for a puppy?" Susannah asked Warwick.

"Yes." Warwick's gaze flitted around those assembled in the small room. He saw Aphrodite shift in her chair, attempting to watch Terpsi as her sister's behavior became more and more outrageous while Callum grew quieter and his gaze colder.

"Yes, I did," Warwick finally answered his sister.

"What do you want with a puppy?"

"I don't want the puppy for myself." Warwick watched Terpsi throw her head back and laugh at a remark from Ridley.

"I thought not, but then why did you send for one?" Susannah's tone became more and more frustrated.

"Because a friend is in need of one."

"Would that friend be Lady Aphrodite?"

"Perhaps I prefer that information to remain between the friend and myself." He raised his eyebrow.

"Don't pull the imperious act on me, Thomas. If you remember, you tottered after me when you were in leading strings. I am hardly likely to be silenced by your noble demeanor now."

He smiled. "All right, the puppy is for Aphrodite. Her scamp of a brother got in trouble. The puppy will help. You might ask your son about his role in the adventure."

"I will do that. I suspected he had been cutting a wheedle but could not get a word out of him." Susannah studied her brother's face. "You are spending a great deal of time with Frederick's future wife."

"She is soon to be a member of our family. We were acquainted in London. I thought it only courteous to renew that acquaintance and welcome her into the family."

"I notice you call her by her first name," Susannah said.

"She is soon to be a cousin. As to the attention paid her, perhaps I am assuming the family duties which will soon be mine, as you have often suggested I do."

"I would think—" Susannah was interrupted by the particularly loud voice of Callum McReynolds, who had stood and strode over to Terpsi.

He took hold of the sagging neckline of her dress and pulled it over her shoulders before he began to shout. "How can you flaunt yourself before the world like this?" His face shone a brilliant red and his deep voice shook.

A dazed Terpsi turned and stared at him, as did everyone in the parlor. A flush rose on her cheeks.

"You display what should be seen only by your husband to men who stare at you with lust in their hearts and passion in their eyes." He shook his finger at Terpsi. "Put on some clothes, woman. Cover your body."

He turned to the two men who sat open-mouthed next to Terpsi to continue the diatribe. "And you, Ridley and Fothergill, if a man loves a woman, he doesn't want her to show other men what belongs to him in marriage. You should be ashamed. All of you." With that, he turned and left the room.

"Oh, my." Aphrodite dashed to her sister and took her hand.

Terpsi hadn't moved since Callum started his harangue, but a smile spread slowly across her features. "I believe he still cares for me, Ditie," she whispered in her sister's ear, in a voice so soft that only one as shameless as Warwick, who had moved closer, could have heard. "Oh, he still loves me, Ditie."

Perhaps that's one burden off her shoulders, Warwick thought. Or one more added.

"I don't think he'd say what he did, that he'd be so upset, if he didn't care about me, Ditie. What do you think?" Terpsi said after she and Aphrodite had reached her chambers only a few minutes later. She danced around her bedroom at the same time she brushed the copper tresses that waved and floated around her.

"Perhaps that's why he was always angry with me. Because he was in love with me and didn't want me flirting with other men." She put down the brush and grinned at herself in the mirror, then whirled to look at Aphrodite. "What do you think?"

"I don't know, but I would think you'd want to wear dresses with a little more conservative neckline if you wish to attract Callum. You could wear a shawl or one of my gowns."

"Oh, Ditie, don't be foolish. If my gowns awaken such a reaction, I'd be a fool to change."

Aphrodite had known Terpsi would say that. It was, after all, exactly the type of reasoning all the other Herringtons would use. She sighed and left her sister's room. As she passed Aski's chambers, a hand grabbed her arm and pulled her inside.

"What have you heard about school? Has Warwick brought the puppy yet?" her brother demanded.

"I don't know, but I feel sure he has looked into procuring the dog. Why are you so anxious?"

"Well, a house party like this is fine for you older people, but Geoffrey and I want to get back to school. To our chums there."

"And the squire's younger daughter?"

"Taking little thing, ain't she?" Aski smoothed his curls back. "Must admit I will miss her, but we are young yet. When she comes out in two or three years, I will go to London and look her up. She needs some town bronze, you know."

Aphrodite smiled at her younger brother. "Yes, you certainly have town bronze."

"Well, I have more than she, but you know I am not ready for the parson's mousetrap. Do not tell me her father would be any happier than Papa if I were to ask for her hand now."

"Yes, darling, you are right." A Herrington using reasoning. Perhaps he was growing up.

"Of course, we could elope. Is Gretna Green to the north?"

But probably not, Aphrodite reflected. "Why don't you ask the squire for a map?" she suggested as she let herself out of the room. When she arrived in her chambers, she allowed Mignon to help her out of her gown and brush her hair, but thoughts tumbled chaotically through her brain.

Aski disguised as an Italian count and Terpsi throwing herself at one man to attract another. These incidents were not unusual. But here she was, the responsible member of the family, considering breaking her possible engagement to a perfectly nice young man because she found him boring and she hated his mother and was more attracted to his cousin, even after he had broken her heart once.

The next morning, Warwick escorted her to the stable to show her a wiggling black puppy who could steal the heart of any young lady.

"She's darling." Aphrodite kneeled to scratch the puppy.

"I shall deliver her this morning and talk to the magistrate to convince him of your brother's innocent intent. I hope that this offering will soften his heart. "Boy," Warwick called to a groom. "Please put the dog in my carriage." The groom rushed to pick up the dog and place it in a box inside the vehicle.

"Thank you." Aphrodite stood. "I cannot tell you how much I appreciate this. And Aski, too." She looked into Warwick's eyes. The sheer power of his eyes held her spellbound. She should look away, she told herself, but she didn't. His gaze didn't waver and warmth filled his eyes. Slowly, he moved toward her until he stood only inches from her.

He took her hand, turned it over and studied her palm for a moment before rubbing his thumb across it, from the base of her thumb across the sensitive skin in the center and up to the tip of her index finger. Then he looked at her with such longing in his eyes that Aphrodite gasped.

The sound seemed to bring him to his senses. He dropped her hand and stepped back. "You will soon be a member of our family. Your brother will be related by marriage, by your marriage to my cousin Frederick." He nodded. "I am glad to be of service," he said with a bow. Then he turned and strode to his carriage, leaped into it, and drove off, leaving billowing dust on the drive.

What had just happened? Aphrodite wondered. Warwick had looked at her with—oh, certainly not love, but what? Desire? How could she, the plain, the dull Herrington, have raised passion in the heart of a man like Warwick? She hadn't raised it in Frederick's heart.

Foolishness, Aphrodite reminded herself. If she knew one thing, she knew that she did not arouse ardor in a man. But, if she didn't, what was that look in his eye?

"Ditie, did he get the dog?"

Aphrodite shook herself and found herself still in the yard outside the stable. Aski ran across the lawn toward her.

"Yes, a lovely puppy. You can return to school."

"Well, I don't want to leave too soon. Geoffrey and I don't want to miss the play, you know."

"I don't care." Aphrodite walked past her brother and toward the house. "Do whatever you decide." She stopped and turned back. "But I do hope you will thank Warwick when he returns. He's gone greatly out of his way for you." She twirled and continued toward Windwillow.

"I don't understand why, Ditie." Aski hurried after her. "Geoffrey says Warwick is the best of fellows, bang up to the nines, but he's not the kind to help other people. This seems most generous of him."

"Yes, it is." They strolled toward the house together.

"Why do you think he got the puppy? And he is delivering it himself, Ditie, and talking to the magistrate. He is going to a lot of trouble. Do you think he wants to court Athena?"

Aphrodite stopped and turned again, almost causing her brother to collide with her. "If you know anything about our little sister, you know a man doesn't have to court her. If he's well set up, perhaps wearing a livery, she is likely to . . ." Aphrodite cut off her words with effort. "No, I do not believe that is the reason. He explained that he did this acting as head of the family, because I'm engaged, almost, to Frederick." She headed toward Windwillow again, with Aski running behind her.

"If that ain't poppycock, I don't know what is. He don't owe me anything."

"Do not refine on it, Aski. Just accept and be grateful."

That afternoon, the guests wandered down to the lake where a picnic had been set up outside the summer house. Susannah sat on a bench in the shade with her younger children. On a bench close to the lake, Athena chatted with Callum, Fothergill, and the squire's daughters while Geoffrey stood behind them and joined in the conversation. Talking and laughing, Terpsi and Hugh Ridley strolled along the shore.

"Come join us," Susannah called and waved to Aphrodite. "Get a glass of lemonade and sit here next to me."

"I wonder when my brother will be back," Susannah said when Aphrodite joined her.

The two women stitched on costumes for a few minutes before Susannah said, "We are to have a great race. Your bro—I mean, Geoffrey's friend Luigi has challenged Geoffrey, Frederick and James to a race, rowing their boats around the lake. I wish Thomas were here to take part."

Aphrodite glanced up to see the men line their boats up on the shore. Her brother, a red scarf tied around his head, his curls bouncing, laughed merrily as he pointed out the route of the race.

"If I may," Frederick came from the shore and bowed before Aphrodite. "Do you have a token that I may carry into the fray?"

With a laugh, Aphrodite picked up a strip of lace from

Susannah's sewing basket and tied it around Frederick's arm.

"Be careful," Athena said to Frederick as he walked back to the boats.

"Of course I will." He got in the boat, then nodded at Athena as he pushed it into the water.

Aphrodite had never found Frederick so attractive. He wore a shirt with the sleeves rolled up to show muscular arms. His face glowed with anticipation and pleasure. Oh, my, for just a moment, her future fiancé made her heart flutter.

"Don't you worry about Mr. Horne's engaging in such a dangerous activity?" Athena frowned as she watched the men.

"Even if I did, Athena, I could not stop him. He wants to do this. Indeed, I believe all the men look delighted."

"Have I missed some sport?" Warwick said.

Aphrodite turned to see him behind her. "The conti has challenged the others to a race. Wouldn't you like to join them?"

"I had a rushed trip, so I'll content myself with watching."

"Oh, tell me how did everything go?" Aphrodite asked.

"I believe the magistrate understands that your brother was not kicking up a lark but was motivated by his deep interest in science and meant no harm." Warwick lowered himself on the bench next to Aphrodite.

"The young lady was very pleased with the puppy. The magistrate says that he will no longer pursue Aski, which means he will be able to return to school."

"As long as Aski is enjoying himself, I imagine it will be difficult to get him to leave, and it is certainly not my responsibility to force him to do so," said Aphrodite.

"Well spoken," Warwick agreed.

"We are off!" shouted Aski. At those words, the men began to row frantically.

"You are not worried that Frederick or your brother are in any danger, are you? I assure you the water is very shallow and Frederick is a good swimmer," Warwick said.

"So is Aski. No, I believe they will be fine, and they are having such a wonderful time."

The men pulled hard on their oars. The boats were close together, the rowers trying to get near to the island to shorten their row.

James' children shouted for their father while the other guests waved their hands and called encouragement to their favorites as the boats disappeared behind the island that blocked their view of the race.

"I cannot tell you how much I appreciate your taking the puppy to the magistrate and rescuing Aski. I hope my disreputable brother is truly grateful."

"I didn't do this for your brother, fair Patience. I hoped to take a slight burden from your shoulders."

Shouts from the group on the shore alerted them to the boats rounding the island. Aski was in front, the other three men close behind as everyone stood to watch the end of the race.

Then disaster struck. Geoffrey tried to overtake Aski, pushing between Frederick and James. To avoid hitting him, Frederick pulled to the left, toward the island. Then Frederick's boat stopped suddenly, and he was thrown over the bow and into the water.

"His boat must have hit something," Warwick shouted as he dashed toward the lake.

Aphrodite searched the water but there was no sight of Frederick. Aski and Geoffrey didn't realize what had happened and continued to row. James attempted to slow his vessel, but it began to spin in the water.

And still she could not see Frederick.

"Freddie!" A woman screamed from the shore.

"Surely the water is too shallow for him to drown," Aphrodite said as she followed Warwick toward the lake.

"It's not deep, but if he's hit his head, he might not be able to stand." Warwick tore off his boots and jacket and started into the water just as Frederick emerged, muddy and sputtering but definitely alive.

"Freddie!" The woman screamed again. Aphrodite looked behind her to discover that the shout came from her younger sister. Athena's face was white. She covered her mouth with her hand while tears rolled down her cheeks.

Warwick strode into the water toward his cousin, grabbed Frederick's arm, and threw it around his neck to help him to the shore.

Aphrodite rushed toward Frederick but, before she reached him, Athena shoved and ran in front of her to stand on the bank, waiting for the two men.

"Freddie!" Athena yelled when he had almost reached the shore. She waded into the water and threw herself into the arms of her sister's fiancé, sobbing. "Oh, Freddie, Freddie. I thought you were dead. I thought you had drowned."

Frederick reacted with great surprise, looking down at the blond head burrowing into his chest. He put his arms around Athena, as if to steady her. Then, for a moment, he held her, a look of such tenderness in his eyes that Aphrodite ached for him.

"Freddie," Athena continued to wail. "Are you really safe?"

Chapter Thirteen

Only Warwick looked at Aphrodite. He glanced back and forth, from Aphrodite to his cousin, who stood with the overwrought Athena attached to him like a limpet.

But the emotional current racing between Aphrodite's intended and her sister lasted for only a second.

After he gained control of himself and recognized the situation, Frederick patted Athena on the back and said, "There, there, little sister. I am fine." He handed the sobbing Athena to Warwick and searched for Aphrodite who stood only a few feet away.

"I will not touch you, Aphrodite." He shook his head and a leaf flew off with a great shower of dirty water. "I would not like to ruin your gown, but I promise I am fine. Completely unhurt, just wet and filthy. I will go to the house to repair this damage." He glanced over his shoulder at Athena, who sobbed into Warwick's ruined neckcloth while he held her gingerly, patting her shoulder occasionally.

Frederick sloshed toward the path to the house while

Warwick looked beseechingly at Aphrodite and Athena hiccuped in his arms.

There was silence. Not one of those gathered around the lake uttered a word as they watched the astonishing scene unfolding before them. Then Aphrodite looked toward them, and everyone began chattering at the same time.

"Is Frederick all right?" Fothergill shouted.

"Yes, fine," Warwick answered.

"Aren't we glad he's all right?" Susannah said loudly.

"What a relief," said Hugh Ridley on top of Susannah's words.

"Oh, my, yes," Terpsi agreed.

"What good luck," the squire added.

The babble of voices continued while Aphrodite beckoned Aski to help her with their sister. Aski put his arm around Athena's waist and she abandoned Warwick to collapse against her new support.

"I'm a friend of the family," Aski explained as if everyone at the house party really believed he was Luigi. "I'm happy to help the family in this emergency."

"May I help?" Callum asked, his plain face filled with concern.

"No, thank you. We will take her to her room and take care of her." Aphrodite took her sister's hand and led her to the path. "Athena has always been very fond of Frederick," she said.

"Very fond," the crowd echoed with nodding heads.

"He will soon be her brother," Warwick stated.

"Oh, yes," they all said.

"I will order a bath." Terpsi dashed ahead of them.

As they started up the path, Aphrodite studied her younger sister. The child's face was streaked with mud from contact with Frederick. Brown water dripped from her hair and the hem of her wet dress, which was molded to her body and made walking difficult. Pieces of her shoes fell off intermittently causing her to use an odd shuffling gait.

This is the girl who screams if a leaf falls on her dress, Aphrodite reflected. Yet, this fastidious young woman had thrown herself into the arms of a man covered with mud and filthy water. Aphrodite knew what this meant, but this was not the time to consider the reasons for her sister's actions. Right now, they had to get her to the house, to warm and comfort her.

Athena sniffled and broke out in loud sobs once they were away from the other guests. "He almost died, Ditie. Frederick almost died."

"But he didn't, Athena. He was very wet, and it was frightening, but if he had not appeared, James and Warwick would have pulled him out before he died."

"Why do you care so much?" Aski demanded. "He ain't your fiancé, he's Ditie's, and she's not fallen into a fit."

"He's . . ." Athena's face showed her struggle to explain her despair.

"She has such a loving heart," Aphrodite said. "You know Athena cannot bear to see anyone hurt."

"Yes." Athena took her hand from her sister's and pushed a limp piece of sodden hair from her own face.

"Oh, Ditie, I'm so miserable."

"I know you are, darling. I'll take care of you."

"What I still don't understand—" Aski began, but Aphrodite silenced him with a kick.

Fifteen minutes later, Athena laid her head on the back of a hip bath and savored the warmth while Aphrodite gathered the ruined clothing together and handed the dripping mess to a maid.

"Let me wash your beautiful hair," Aphrodite said as she settled in a chair she'd pulled beside the bath.

"You're so good to me, Ditie." Tears continued to flow.

"Now, now, don't cry. You'll make yourself sick." Aphrodite began to lather Athena's curls. "Just let me get all this dirty water out, and then we'll dry your hair and you'll feel so much better." She poured a pan of warm water over her sister's head then wrapped it in a towel.

But the tears still streamed down her face. Aphrodite took out her handkerchief and dabbed at Athena's eyes. "Don't worry, darling. You rest, then we'll talk about this. You know we can always solve problems together."

"Oh, but not this one, Ditie. Not this one." The sobs shook Athena's body.

"Oh, yes, even this. We can work this out together."

"You are so good, Ditie, and I am so miserable." Athena's voice shook.

"Come, darling." Aphrodite helped her sister from the tub and enfolded her in a heavy robe. "You sit here, and I'll brush your hair while it dries. That always makes you feel better." As she coddled Athena, she realized she had again fallen into her natural place, taking care of her madcap and heedless family. Well, she reasoned, this is an emergency.

Athena's eyelids drooped as warmth and her sister's soothing presence comforted her. When she had finished with Athena's hair, Aphrodite helped her out of the robe and into a nightgown, then placed her in bed and covered her with a quilt.

Three hours later, after she too had bathed, rested, and dressed for dinner, Aphrodite took Mignon to Athena's room where Terpsi awaited them outside the door.

"Time to get up." Aphrodite shook her sister. "Dinner will be announced shortly."

"Oh, Ditie, I can't go to dinner. I can never face any of these people again. I behaved so foolishly." Athena's face was still pale and tears threatened to overflow.

"Now, darling, the longer you stay away from the guests, the harder it will be."

Terpsi took Athena's hand. "You know how many embarrassing things I've done, Athena."

"Oh my, yes," Athena agreed. "Hundreds."

"Each time, I discovered that facing those who witnessed your mortification immediately was much easier than wondering how they would behave."

"Don't forget, you have your family here, and we all love you." Aphrodite took Athena's hand and pulled her from the bed.

"You are too good to me," Athena whispered.

Aphrodite couldn't help but feel sorry for Athena, even knowing that her younger sister had fallen in love with Frederick. Athena's throwing herself in the arms of a wet, dirty man took as much courage as it would for Aphrodite to throw herself in front of a bullet. It could only have come from love, a depth of love Aphrodite had not thought her little sister capable of.

When the sisters entered the parlor, all eyes turned toward them, then away just as quickly. Athena paused, but Terpsi and Aphrodite exchanged a quick glance and pulled her into the room.

"Come here, girl." Mrs. Horne pointed at Athena as she pounded her stick on the floor.

"Me?" Athena whispered.

"You. The yella-headed one."

"I'll be right here beside you," Aphrodite said.

While Athena moved hesitantly toward the behemoth ensconced in her enormous brown chair, Mrs. Horne leaned forward to peer at Athena.

"What did I hear about you this afternoon, girl?" She turned to Frederick. "Didn't I hear this chit went into the water when you fell in?"

When no one answered, Mrs. Horne continued speaking to her son. "Is she as stupid as she looks? Only a fool would go wading in that water when she don't have to."

"Mother." Frederick's voice was low and steady, his words carefully enunciated. "Lady Athena is a guest in this house. I expect you to treat her with courtesy and kindness."

Mrs. Horne turned back to Athena. "Well, girl, what do you have to say?"

"Mother, have I not made myself clear?" Frederick asked firmly.

Mrs. Horne's face froze. Her small eyes glittered as she ran her tongue over her lower lip. She glanced up at her son, then, with a sigh, she sat back in the chair. "Come here, child. It must have been a terrible experience. Sit here next to me and tell me about it."

Everyone gasped in surprise as Athena joined Mrs. Horne for a comfortable coze before the roaring fire. When the older woman took Athena's hand and patted it, the guests could barely take in the amazing change in the harridan.

Aphrodite watched to make sure the ogre treated her sensitive little sister in a civil manner, but the *tête-à-tête* progressed politely as Athena prattled away.

That evening, once the house was quiet, Aphrodite stepped into the dark hall and found her way to Athena's room. She opened the door to discover the room dark and her sister asleep.

With a sense of relief that the conversation could be put off, Aphrodite went back to her room, slipped into a robe, and attempted to calm her thoughts.

What was to become of her? she wondered as she tugged the brush through her hair. It was a selfish consideration, she knew. It was equally obvious Athena and Frederick cared deeply for each other, but neither wanted to hurt her. How foolish.

She would work that out. After all, her younger sister

would be rescued from her flirtatious tendencies and now would be held safe in the love of a good man.

Although Athena's problems seemed to be resolved, Aski still disguised himself as an Italian count and Terpsi continued to throw herself at one man to attract another and, of course, Aphrodite herself had lost her fiancé. She did not look forward to having society know what had happened at Windwillow. What would people say?

What more could go wrong? she asked herself, and fell asleep with those unanswered questions whirling through her mind.

Chapter Fourteen

Never ask such a thing, never tempt fate, Aphrodite scolded herself the next day when quite possibly the worst event she ever could have imagined came about.

While Terpsi fidgeted with a neckline that threatened to fall off both shoulders at once, Callum wore a frown that seemed to be carved into his forehead. Aski, in a brilliant orange jacket with matching ribbons around his head, danced through the group as an outrageous and completely out-of-control Puck. Both of the squire's daughters laughed and chased after him. A few feet from Terpsi stood Athena, surreptitiously studying Frederick from lowered eyes as she pretended to study her lines.

Frederick leaned stiffly against a wall of the ballroom, not far from the group, and watched while Susannah stitched on the costumes. Seated on the edge of the stage, James, Fothergill, and Warwick discussed the merits of a chestnut they'd seen at Tattersall's.

Watching it all, Aphrodite wondered if she should shake Terpsi, trip Aski, or comfort Athena, although she had no idea what bothered her younger sister at this moment. She could feel the furrows between her brows grow deeper.

After Terpsi and Callum had shouted their lines at each other and Puck had spoken his verses, Aphrodite and Warwick stood to begin their parts.

When they finished their part of the scene, she and Warwick sat on the settee next to Susannah, and Aphrodite picked up a costume to sew.

"You are both very good actors." Susannah cut a thread.

"Thank you." Aphrodite eyed her stitches.

"One would almost think," Susannah said as she sewed. "One would almost think, if one didn't know you better, that there really is an attraction, a strong attraction, between the two of you. Not, of course, that you flirt. It merely seems that way."

Aphrodite stared at her friend. The tone of Susannah's voice reminded her of how Terpsi, when she wanted to meddle in other people's private thoughts, would state a fact but disguise it as a comment, an opinion, or even a question.

"Yes," Warwick said. "One might say that. Or, one might say we are fine actors."

His voice, Aphrodite thought, sounded too much like the sibling on the receiving end of her judgment, who understood what was insinuated and denied it, but not successfully. Why did he sound defensive? There was nothing to deny on his part.

"Everyone!" Mrs. Horne shouted as she entered the ballroom. She waved her cane at Frederick, who hurried to his mother so she could lean on his arm. "I have a surprise for you." Then she stepped back.

The Marquis and Marchioness of Temple stood behind her.

"Mama! Papa!" Athena dashed to her parents. After she

hugged them both, she turned to her siblings. "Isn't it wonderful? Mama and Papa are here."

Aphrodite embraced both parents. "What a delightful surprise." Of course more could go wrong. The only thing worse than having the Herrington siblings fall into all their usual multitude of scrapes was for their parents to witness them. No, Aphrodite thought, far worse was that she had joined her imprudent siblings in their folly this time.

Aphrodite glanced over her shoulder. Aski had attempted to hide behind the plants, and Terpsi had pulled her dress up to her neck and held it in place with both hands.

Of all of the siblings, only Athena looked completely innocent with her blue eyes wide and happy.

"What brings you here?" Aphrodite asked.

"We had to come, darling." Hazel kissed Aphrodite and Athena. "This is a most important time for you, dear Ditie. I talked your father into allowing us to travel here, little by little. Mrs. Horne was so lovely about entering into the spirit of our little surprise. How marvelous that you will have such a sweet *belle-mère*." She nodded regally toward Mrs. Horne.

"Now, let me see my other darlings. Terpsi?" The marchioness turned toward the group and held out her hands. When Terpsi stood, attempting to pull the neckline of her dress up to her chin, her mother gasped. Although Hazel possessed what could only be termed haphazard ideas about rearing children, she would not allow her daughters to tarnish their reputations.

"For heaven's sake, child, go put on some clothes." The marchioness spoke in a voice that allowed no argument and pointed to the door. "Do it *now*, my darling daughter."

Terpsi kissed her parents' cheeks before dashing from the room.

"Aski," his father said. "Are you hiding from me? What are you doing back there in that ridiculous costume?"

Aski stood. "It's a lark, Papa."

"And for how long have you missed school?" The marquis strode toward his son.

"For two weeks, Papa."

"For two entire weeks? We will deal with that later."

The color drained from Aski's face. "Yes, sir."

"What have you done with your hair?" The marquis circled Aski, looking at the curls with disbelief.

When his son didn't answer, the marquis continued, "For the moment, you will comb your hair, then remove that terrible jacket and throw it away. When you return, you will be dressed as a Herrington dresses in company."

"Yes, sir." Aski kissed his mother's cheek as he left.

"Please continue with what you were doing," Hazel said with a smile as she settled into one of the comfortable chairs a footman had provided for them, between her husband and Mrs. Horne. "The marquis and I will just watch."

"Yes, yes." The marquis waved his hand. "Please continue." He moved his chair closer to his wife's, leaned on the armrest they both shared, and placed his hand on hers.

"Now," said Mrs. Horne as she sat beside them. "Do tell me all about your family. How many children do you have?"

"Tell me all about what has happened at this wonderful house party." The marchioness settled on the sphinx sofa of cherry-striped satin for a chat with Aphrodite that afternoon. She patted the seat for her daughter to join her.

"Well—" Aphrodite paused to consider. Should she begin with Athena's stealing her unwanted fiancé? Or, perhaps, Aski's foolishness, although she had no doubt her father had already uncovered that. She could mention the feud Terpsi carried on with her former beau. Or she could tell her mother that she would break her own engagement because she had developed a powerful passion for a man who had once before played her false.

"It has been fairly uneventful," Aphrodite said. "We are putting on *A Midsummer Night's Dream.* Terpsi is in charge."

"Of course. And you and Frederick are one of the pairs of lovers?"

"Well, it started out that way. Athena and Warwick were to be Hermia and Lysander, but he frightened her, so we traded."

"And so you are paired with Warwick while she is with Frederick?" The marchioness pondered this. "Well, it sounds like a nice time. How do you find Mrs. Horne? She was so pleased to help us."

"Frederick is devoted to her."

"My dear, I cannot tell you how proud your father and I are of you." Hazel patted her daughter on the knee.

"You are proud? Of me? Whatever for?"

"You are our responsible child, our only responsible child, although Ceto shows a disturbing tendency in that direction. Time will tell." Hazel paused to reorder her thoughts.

"You were so different from the rest of us," she continued. "We had no idea how to act when you were growing up. But, look at you! You've done marvelously. You are to marry a most unexceptionable young man with a lovely estate and a nice fortune. And he's loving and loyal to his mother. That shows he will also treat his wife well. We are delighted. That's why I felt we had to be here to share this important time with you, to be here when you announced your engagement. Of course, your father has to take care of the settlements with Frederick, but I wanted to be here to celebrate with you."

"Thank you, Mama. I don't know what to say." She knew she'd be at an equal loss for words when she had to explain that Athena, not Aphrodite, would marry Frederick. Instead of saying anything, she kissed the marchioness on the cheek.

How could she mention her attraction to Warwick when her mother considered her the one responsible member of the family? How could she contemplate breaking her expected engagement while her parents beamed proudly at her? Well, there was no choice about that, even if it meant she had to explain she had fallen in love with a man even her parents recognized as a rake. But she could no longer go on being the good daughter who gave up everything for her madcap siblings.

"Is there anything you would like to tell me?" her mother asked.

Aphrodite looked up into eyes filled with concern. "No, nothing," she lied.

"Well, your father and I are very pleased," her mother repeated. "I see that Warwick is here. Have you become acquainted with him?"

"He is representing his father here."

"So I would imagine. Have you become acquainted with him?"

"Yes. He is, after all, playing Demetrius and I am Helena, so we are together often in the play."

"And, have you gotten better acquainted with him?"

"Yes, he is a fine actor and has learned most of his lines."

"That is very interesting." Hazel studied Aphrodite's face for a moment. "Now, let me ring for some tea. Then you tell me all about this Frederick and his mother. Did you know that she has set up a delightful evening of dancing for our entertainment tonight? Your father and I do so enjoy dancing."

"Yes, Mama. I am aware of that."

* * *

"I believe your fiancé has fallen in love with your sister," Warwick said as he and Aphrodite danced together that evening.

Mrs. Horne had planned a lovely party. The doors of two parlors had been thrown open to accommodate the seven couples as the squire's wife played a country dance on the piano.

Aphrodite looked up at her partner, who looked uncharacteristically serious, the sparkle missing from his deep blue eyes.

"I find that difficult to believe," Aphrodite said as she followed the steps of the country dance. She studied Frederick and Athena across the parlors, then continued as the music brought them back together. "Frederick would never be able to introduce Athena to his mother as his future bride."

"Why not?"

"Certainly you realize that Mrs. Horne would never countenance a Mad Herrington as a daughter."

"And yet she accepted you, fair Patience." Warwick turned to the left, then moved with the steps of the dance back toward Aphrodite.

"As you well know, I am not considered to be one of the Mad Herringtons. In fact, people often state they believe I must be a changeling in this family."

"Levelheaded, not one to give in to passion and the temptation of the moment? A pity. Do you and Frederick agree on the need to be levelheaded and composed?"

He smiled at her, the smile that she guessed had caused the hearts of women far more sophisticated than she to leap in their breasts. Hers followed suit, but she acted unaffected. She moved away with the steps of the dance, fearing he could hear or feel its vibrations.

"My engagement is none of your concern."

"As a member of the family, I am concerned that you and your prospective groom will be happy together."

"As you know, Frederick and I share many common interests and are comfortable," she said. "Were we to marry, I believe we would live contentedly."

" 'Were' you to marry? Do you contemplate ending the engagement?"

"We never have been formally engaged, as you know, but I believe Frederick's wife will have a comfortable, serene life."

"Dear Patience, you do not value yourself highly enough. I cannot believe you'd be happy with a comfortable life. You are more of a Mad Herrington than you believe."

She attempted to study him coolly, as the Aphrodite of a few weeks ago would have done without effort, yet she felt anything but detached when she was with him.

"Your passionate nature is reflected in your eyes. They flash and sparkle."

"It is? They do?" Aphrodite looked away, startled. Certainly the man couldn't read how she felt, could he? But he was a connoisseur of women. Perhaps he could. She stumbled, but Warwick grasped her arm and kept her from falling.

Aphrodite could tell she was succumbing to the dangerous pull of his charm and tried to think of something to say.

"And your hair," Warwick continued. "It is the most unusual color I've ever seen. Auburn and blond, mixed together. Glorious. It is burnished gold in the sunlight."

Thank goodness she was sensible to an inordinate degree, Aphrodite thought, or she would have thrown herself into his arms. "I do not believe there is anything special about my hair."

Warwick took a tendril of her hair that had escaped from her tightly coiled coiffure and wound it around his finger.

"You shouldn't keep it pulled back that way. It should be loose, waving and curling down your back."

"That is not a proper hair style." A delicate flush spread across her cheeks as she turned away. "It is Athena who has the beautiful hair."

Unfortunately, the mention of her sister made her look toward where Athena stood with Frederick. "She has that lovely pale hair that everyone admires."

As they watched, Athena tossed her head and shook her silver blond tresses while Frederick stood with his hands held behind his back and his eyes firmly fixed on a spot a few inches above Athena's head. But, when the steps of the dance turned Warwick away, Aphrodite saw Frederick's eyes dart in Athena's direction for only a moment, his body leaning toward the young woman with yearning, before he again studied the wall behind her. Hardly the emotion one expects of one's fiancé for one's sister, Aphrodite reflected.

As the steps of the dance again parted them, Aphrodite noticed that Terpsi, much more modestly attired in a high-necked gown of Sardinian blue sarsenet with a striped slip, laughed up at Hugh Ridley while Callum, who had earlier danced with Susannah, now stood up with Gwendolyn.

They had danced in silence for a few moments when Warwick said, "When will you and Frederick announce your betrothal? I believe the purpose for the ball on Saturday is to announce your impending marriage."

Again, Aphrodite lost track of the steps of the dance. She stood still for a moment, motionless amid the flow of dancers moving around her and her partner.

"No," she said. "I'm not sure," she babbled. "Perhaps, but possibly not. At least, not then." She looked up at Warwick and thought she saw a softness in his eyes. Was it compassion?

Warwick took her hand and pulled her into the flow of the dance while Aphrodite contemplated how close the future was and how little prepared she was for whatever would happen.

Then the music stopped and he led her back to where her parents sipped arack and nibbled on lemon biscuits.

"Do get yourself something to eat, darling," the marchioness said. "Mrs. Horne's cook has prepared a wonderful selection." She waved toward their hostess, seated at a table and gobbling down delicious morsels.

"My lady." Warwick bowed toward the marchioness, then led her out to dance.

Ignoring Hugh Ridley, who had started to bow in front of her, Aphrodite slipped out the French door and tiptoed down the stairs and into the garden, where she settled onto a solitary bench hidden by a row of carefully clipped yews.

This is Wednesday, she thought. In only a few days, she was supposed to announce her engagement to a man who was in love with her sister. Never mind the fact that she didn't love him nor that she cared for a man who had proven himself fickle before. She would have to do something.

And ruin her parents' vision—and her own—of Aphrodite as the responsible Herrington.

But what if Athena's thoughts were as confused as Terpsi's? Was it possible that Athena was pretending to be in love with Frederick to attract Warwick? She had, after all, stated that Frederick was an old stick and had wondered what Warwick's kisses would be like.

But could Athena have pretended her fright when Frederick fell into the water or her relief when he emerged unharmed? Or had she done that because Warwick had just joined the group by the lake?

Aphrodite sighed again. Who knew what her muddlebrained family really thought about anything? She must interrogate Athena carefully to straighten this coil out.

* * *

"Hello, darling." Aphrodite entered her younger sister's chambers that night after the guests had retired.

Athena turned on the bench in front of the Egyptian dressing glass where she had been studying her reflection. She waved the maid away.

"Yes, Ditie?" she said with a quavering smile.

"Darling, I love you." Aphrodite sat on the bed. "I want what's best for you, but you have to tell me the truth."

"The truth, Ditie? About what?" Athena began to brush her hair.

"I believe you are in love with Frederick and it is obvious he returns your feelings."

Athena looked at her sister, her face glowing with joy. "Oh, Ditie, do you think he does? I thought so but I wasn't sure. He's so quiet and honorable and covers his feelings." A soft smile hovered on her lips. "I couldn't tell. He doesn't give me compliments or try to kiss me like all the other men." She paused. "I shouldn't have said that, Ditie. I did not want to fall in love with your fiancé. I really did not mean to."

"I know, and I'm surprised. You thought him dull only a short time ago."

"I didn't know him." Her face took a bemused and slightly unfocused look. "Frederick isn't boring. He's reliable. Trustworthy. He makes me feel protected and safe." Athena smiled dreamily at her sister. "Most men make me feel stupid, but Frederick doesn't. He likes me, as a person. He seems to enjoy talking to me, not just looking at me."

"That must be very nice, dear. Do you want to marry him?"

"Oh, Ditie, how could I? You're engaged to him. Almost."

"You cannot think I would be happy, married to the man you love, and who seems to care about you."

Athena's eyes flew open. "Are you sure? What makes you think he could love me?"

Aphrodite put her hand on Athena's. "Little sister, I saw his face when you ran to him when he came out of the water, and I saw it again when you were together this evening."

"What did he look like, Ditie?"

"He looked like a man who was trying to show that he did not love you, like a man trying to be loyal to the woman he is to marry."

"You think he loves me?"

"I first guessed how much he cares for you when he refused to allow his mother to mistreat you."

"He did, didn't he?"

"My dear, why would I want to marry him if he loves you?"

Athena started to throw her arms around her sister, but Aphrodite stopped her with an upheld hand. "Athena, there is one more thing. If you were married, you couldn't kiss other men."

"Oh, Ditie, you think I'm such a widgeon. Of course I wouldn't kiss other men. It would hurt Frederick's feelings. Besides, if I were married to Frederick, I wouldn't want to kiss anyone else."

"Are you sure?"

"Well, fairly sure. I have not kissed him, but I think it would be very pleasant. Did you kiss Frederick? Did you like it?" Athena leaned forward.

"I hardly think . . ."

"It would not be wrong if you kissed him. You are, after all, almost engaged."

"But not likely ever to marry."

"Well," Athena continued, her eyes becoming dreamy again as she leaned back against the table. "I think if I liked to kiss Frederick, and I *do* think I would, I believe no other man would appeal to me. You know—" she looked at her sister seriously. "I kissed all those other men because I wanted to know how it felt to love and to be loved, but now I know that love is far more than just cuddling and kisses."

"Well, you seem to have grown up." Aphrodite stood. "Just one more thing, and it seems foolish. Nonetheless, I have to ask. You're not just pretending to love Frederick to make Warwick jealous?"

Athena blinked. "Why would I do that? That's foolish. Oh." She thought for a moment. "That's what Terpsi is doing, isn't it? Trying to make Callum jealous. Well, no, I wouldn't. I'm not a complete cawker. Besides, why would I want Warwick when it's obvious that you and he are perfect for each other?"

"Hardly so." Aphrodite started toward the door.

"Ditie, I am sorry."

"Why, darling?" She turned to face her sister.

"I have to confess. I am not completely innocent, Ditie. I did flirt with Frederick, just a little."

"I am sure you did, darling. I would be surprised to know that you didn't flirt with a man."

"But I tried to stop, Ditie. I was afraid I was making him fall in love with me. Men do, except Warwick. I didn't mean to take Frederick from you. I hope I didn't hurt you too much."

"No, darling. It's a little confusing and unsettling, but not the least bit painful." Except, she thought, to her confidence.

"I didn't think you really cared about Frederick. You seemed comfortable with him, nothing more. Besides, this is best. You belong with Warwick."

"Athena . . ."

"I told you that weeks ago, Ditie. You never believed

me." When her sister didn't speak, Athena added, "What are we going to do, Ditie?"

"Don't worry. I will try to find time to speak to Frederick tomorrow, to let him know he is free to court you."

"Oh, Ditie, you are the most wonderful sister." Athena jumped to her feet and hugged Aphrodite. "I love you."

"I love you, too." She patted her younger sister on the back. "Now, go to bed. Everything will be fine, darling."

Everything would be fine for Athena and Frederick, but how would she tell her parents they would celebrate the engagement not of their responsible daughter but of her irresponsible younger sister? she wondered as she entered her chambers. How would she tell them that the coquette was to marry, not the older daughter who would soon be on the shelf.

She peered at herself in the mirror. If Frederick did not find her attractive, why would Warwick? She doubted it herself, in spite of his honeyed words.

That night as she changed into her night rail and slipped into bed, she refused to ask what more could go wrong. The answer was only too obvious. Everything.

Stretched out on the bed, the marquis studied his wife as he had every night for the past twenty-six years as she brushed her hair one hundred times in front of the mirror.

His beloved chewed her lip, a sign of agitation that he needed to calm. He stood and moved to the mirror where he put his hands on her neck and began to rub her shoulders. "What worries you, my love?" he asked.

"The children." Hazel sighed.

"Well, of course the children. Terpsi?"

"Oh, no. Her outrageous behavior is to be expected. She has never forgotten Mr. McReynolds so is attempting to attach him again. Why she believes flaunting herself is the answer, I do not know. No, I understand Terpsi, although I shan't allow her to behave like a strumpet."

"Then is it Athena?"

"Oh, no. Neither of her sisters would allow her to ruin herself. However," she said as she turned to look up at him, "we do need to find a husband for her soon."

"Then it must be Aski who worries you."

"No, my dear. He is foolish, but he is young. Were you ever such a loose screw, Clive?"

"If I was, I didn't consider myself foolish. Perhaps half-flash. By the time we met, I considered myself quite dashing."

"Oh, you were, and Aski will be, but he must return to school."

"I will see that he is there by Sunday." The marquis sat on the end of the bed. "You cannot be worried about Aphrodite."

"Oh, yes, Clive, I am."

"But she has always behaved properly. Why do you worry?"

"Because she does not look happy, and because it is past time for her to behave just a bit improperly. She doesn't know how." Hazel paused. "What I saw today worries me. I saw her look at Warwick, and he at her. There is something between the two of them. I would not want her to be hurt. If she marries Mr. Horne, she will miss out on all you and I have shared. But if she refuses Mr. Horne, would Warwick offer for her?"

"And how did Warwick look at Ditie?"

"He looked at her as you look at me. With passion but also, I believe, with love."

"Then do not refine on this, dearest. Ditie is surely old enough to decide what she wants."

"But Warwick and our Ditie?"

"You remember what our parents said when I told them

I wished to offer for you? My parents laughed because I was so young. Yours worried and almost did not allow me to speak to you because of my reputation."

"But you were young, not jaded. Warwick is nearly thirty. He may be set in his rakish ways."

"And you, my love, were as naughty a puss as London had seen, but we have been happily and lovingly married for years. There has never been another woman for me. Perhaps Warwick only needs to fall in love to change."

Chapter Fifteen

Aphrodite stood at the door of the breakfast parlor. Frederick sat across the table from Warwick, eating a piece of toast. Both men were absorbed in their newspapers.

With a deep breath, she squared her shoulders and entered the room. Both men stood. "Good morning," she said. She placed a muffin on her plate and poured herself a cup of tea then approached the table.

Warwick nodded a good morning, then sat and returned to his newspaper after Aphrodite settled in a chair next to Frederick.

"How lovely to see you," Frederick said. "My mother wished to sleep later, so I am able to join you for breakfast."

She sipped her tea then spread marmalade onto her muffin. She felt greatly relieved that she didn't have to face those inquisitive eyes of Warwick's that interpreted her expressions and actions so well. However, he made his presence known from behind the newspaper that rattled whenever he turned a page. Once or twice, he peered over the top of it, but she ignored him. While the three of them ate, Warwick interrupted the silence to read a few items of interest to which Frederick responded.

When Frederick finished his coffee, Warwick still had not left the table, although, as far as Aphrodite could tell, he had finished his breakfast even before she entered. Obviously, she and Frederick could not have a private conversation here.

As Frederick stood to take his leave, Aphrodite said, "Frederick, I wonder if we could take a walk this morning."

"That would be delightful." Frederick motioned for the footman to pour more tea for her. "I must meet with my man of business shortly. If your sister will excuse us from our practice, I will meet you at ten in the entrance hall. There are gardens you haven't seen yet I would like to show you."

Aphrodite nodded. "Terpsi changed the rehearsal times. Our last one is after luncheon." She watched her soon-to-be-no-longer fiancé walk from the breakfast parlor, abandoning her.

Warwick's raised eyebrow appeared as he lowered the newspaper. With great haste, she patted her mouth with the napkin, dropped it on the table, and stood, hoping to leave before he could speak. She was within an instant of breaking free when she heard him.

"Ah," he said before she could quite escape.

She turned. "Yes?"

"Oh, nothing. Just noting that you and Frederick are going on a walk. Is there anything special you plan to discuss?"

"The topic of our conversation concerns only Frederick and me." She spun and started into the hall when his words again stopped her.

"Of course," Warwick said. "But I just wondered about, well, you know."

Curiosity stopped her again. "*What* did you wonder about?" she said over her shoulder.

"If what you are discussing has anything to do with our conversation of last night."

"Why would you believe that? Frederick and I have many topics to discuss, private topics." She strode down the hall. If she were determined to keep Warwick from knowing the subject of the conversation with Frederick, why was it so difficult not to pause when he spoke?

"I thought, perhaps, it did." His voice followed her down the hall.

Once in her chambers, Aphrodite considered writing a letter to her parents before she remembered, with a groan, that they were here, that very possibly her father planned to meet Frederick that day to decide on the marriage settlements. Well, he could arrange them for Athena.

Instead, she wrote a short letter to her youngest siblings, illustrated with a silly picture of Aski rowing around the lake. By the time she had pulled on her gloves and tied on a bonnet with ribbons that matched the spring green of her morning gown, it was ten o'clock.

"How lovely you look." Frederick smiled when he saw her on the stairs. He climbed to the landing to offer his arm.

When Aphrodite placed her hand on his arm, she considered him. What a nice, steady man, she thought. Perfect for Athena. "Did you look in on your mother? Is she feeling better?"

"She's still feeling a bit out of curl. I believe if she rests all day, she'll be right as a trivet by our performance this evening." Frederick placed his hand over Aphrodite's.

They strolled to the southwest corner of the house to a bench that overlooked a lovely garden.

Aphrodite turned and said, "Frederick?"

He looked at her with a gentle smile. "Ah, yes, what did you wish to talk to me about?"

"What are your feelings for my sister Athena?"

Frederick's eyes shifted away and he studied the buttons on his cuff as if they were precious heirlooms.

"She is a lovely young woman," he said after nearly a minute. "A delightful young woman to have in my family, as my wife's sister."

"Would you say she is intelligent?"

"Of course not, but of a sweet, loving nature."

"You find her of a sweet, *loving* nature, Frederick?"

He snapped his gaze up at Aphrodite, looking both angry and chagrined. How was it possible to do both? she wondered.

"I do not know to what you refer. She is your sister, so, of course, I feel a . . ." He paused to search for the word. "A purely brotherly interest in her."

"Frederick, please be truthful. Do you love Athena? As a man loves a woman?"

"Why would you ask, my dear? Have I been neglecting you again?" He took her hand. "I am sorry. I have had to spend more time with your sister because of the drama, but I promise I will be more attentive. I do not want Warwick to ring a peal over me again." He stood and helped her to her feet, although she didn't want to stand. "Now, let us take a walk through the garden. Please tell me how you feel about the tea roses mother is having planted."

But Aphrodite sat on a bench and pulled Frederick beside her. "Frederick, please. Are you in love with my sister?"

He settled himself on the bench again. "My dear, you must know that I am a man of honor. I will not cry off. After your father and I have met, we will announce our engagement as planned, tomorrow evening."

"And so, you do not love my sister?"

"I have said that I do not."

"What a bouncer, Frederick. I have seen you look at her and she at you. I believe you do care for her, but as an honorable man, will not break our not-yet-settled engagement."

He looked over her head and said nothing.

"If you do not care for her, you must be aware that she has a *tendre* for you."

He did not answer, but a smile hovered around his lips.

"Do you really believe that I would marry a man my sister loves? A man who returns her love? What a bumble broth that would make. Frederick, do you love my sister?"

He continued to study something behind Aphrodite, emotions she could not read flitting across his face. Finally, he looked into Aphrodite's eyes. "Yes, but I do not wish to hurt you."

"The only way you could hurt me is if you did not tell me the truth. I release you and wish you and Athena happy."

Frederick smiled, a smile of such sweetness and joy that Aphrodite could have been cast down by his delight about their broken engagement. Although she didn't want to marry him any more than he wished to marry her, it would have been nice had he looked a trifle sad.

"Then you and I shall not announce our engagement tomorrow. Shall I announce that we are no longer contemplating an engagement?" he asked.

"Oh, please, no. I wish you would not mention the change in our relationship until we return to London. And, please delay fixing your interest with Athena until then. Such a disclosure would embarrass me, would discomfit everyone here. They would be confused—happy for you and Athena; hearty and bracing toward me. I would not desire that."

"Of course, my dear. Thank you for being so understanding. I had thought you and I would have a very comfortable life together. Imagine my surprise when I fell in love." He shook his head, then looked at Aphrodite, his face mirroring his wonder. "And, as pleasant as parts of this are, I also discover that love is not at all comfortable."

"Especially not when one is engaged to marry another woman."

Well, that is finished, Aphrodite thought with relief and sorrow. She held Frederick's gaze and said, "There is one other thing." She considered her words. "I truly realized that you cared for Athena when you protected her from your mother's tongue. You never did that for me, Frederick."

"I apologize." He did look dismayed and took Aphrodite's hand. "I had not thought you needed to be defended. My mother is a most loving woman but occasionally expresses herself strongly, and your sister is a delicate flower." He paused, "Not, of course, that you are not a delicate flower, but Lady Athena seemed so upset by my mother's remarks."

Aphrodite pulled her hands away from him and held one up to stop the flow of words. "Then, this is the promise you must make to me. You must continue to protect her. That is the only favor I ask. You must never let your mother hurt her."

"I promise." He stood and helped her to her feet. "What will you do, Aphrodite?"

"I shan't wear the willow for you," she said with spirit. "I believe I shall find enough to keep busy."

But, as they returned to the house together in silence, she felt blue-deviled, oddly so considering she had terminated an engagement that neither of them desired.

Her life had always revolved around her family, but she had discovered that was not enough. For several weeks, she had thought her future was sure, but now it was unknown.

All very well to flirt with Warwick when safely engaged

to Frederick, to enjoy the *frisson* his glance and touch excited, but she knew better than to expect anything more than a delightful flirtation with Warwick. She could not expect an offer of marriage from him, after he'd avoided the parson's mousetrap successfully for all these years. The responsible Herrington was hardly the woman to change his mind and heart.

Would she decline into a hatchet-faced maiden aunt who took delight in her siblings' children while she had none of her own? The thought was lowering.

"Do you mind if I talk to the gardener?" Frederick asked when they had reached the steps leading up to the house. "Susannah asked me to make sure that certain plants are ready for this afternoon and evening, and I need to discuss this with him."

"Go ahead. I shall be fine," she said. A nice man, thoroughly admirable, and he raised not a bit of passion in her, she thought as he walked away.

She should be delighted she would not have to spend the rest of her life under the thumb of Matilda Horne or to contemplate spending the rest of her life with a husband who was in love with her own sister, Aphrodite lectured herself. But when she contemplated the uncertainty of her future, she was overset. Tears threatened to fall when she entered the front hall alone.

Then she saw Warwick standing in the entrance hall. Was he waiting for her? Couldn't he leave her be? Did he wish to make sport of her plight?

That was not fair. He had almost always been pleasant, but she didn't want to face him or his questions. She lifted her chin and prepared to do battle.

"How was your conversation?" Warwick asked.

"I do not understand why you have been so rag-mannered about this," she answered, more short-tempered than she'd meant to be. "Certainly, I can take a walk with Frederick without having to explain it to you."

"Certainly, you can. I am just showing interest, in the family, you understand."

He looked down at her. Really, she wished she could throw herself on his chest and cry out her vexation, but he would probably push her away and complain that she had ruined his perfect neckcloth and she'd feel like such a looby. No, that wasn't fair at all. He'd been all consideration for her, and she had no right to cut up at him.

"Poor honey," he said. "Do not forget who stands your friend."

"Thank you." Confused at his concern, she dashed for the stairs, then stopped at the first landing and turned to look down at him. He was watching her.

"Do not forget, fair Helena, the last practice is after our luncheon. We perform tonight." He bowed, then turned and went out the door.

She trudged up the remainder of the steps. First she knocked on the door of Athena's room.

"Yes, Ditie?" Athena bit her lip as she opened the door to her sister. She sat on the bench of the dressing table and twisted the tassels of her sleeve between her fingers.

"Do not worry, love," Aphrodite said. "I have broken my engagement with Frederick."

"Oh, Ditie." Athena's face glowed.

"I have asked Frederick not to say anything until the house party is over, neither that we are not to marry or that you and he may."

"Oh, Ditie, he does wish to marry me?"

"You and he will have to discuss that, but, pray, not until we return to London."

When she left the room, Aphrodite thought she might lie down. Breaking an engagement was an exhausting task. A tisane might be nice to take care of the megrim that threatened. But when she arrived at her bedroom, her mother was settled in a chair by the window, embroidering a cover for a fire screen.

"Hello, Mama," she said as she kissed her on the cheek. "How good to see you. I do need to talk to you. I have just told Frederick that we do not suit."

"Oh, my dear, I am so sorry. We all believed your future was decided." Hazel wrapped her daughter in her arms and allowed her to cry. "There is another man for you, my dear," her mother comforted her. "You will return to London and find a man who will make you happier than Frederick."

With that remark, Aphrodite cried even harder because she had found that man. He was at Windwillow, but he would never ask her to marry him.

When Athena and Aphrodite entered the ballroom three hours later, the younger sister danced and frolicked.

"Look, Ditie, isn't the stage lovely."

Indeed, it was. Susannah, James, Aski, and Hugh Ridley had transformed it into a forest. Ivy climbed the lattice that served as the backdrop and a large tree Susannah's children had drawn hung from a chandelier, brushing its roots on the stage.

"And that," Terpsi said pointing behind the tree where gauzy fabric hung, "*that* is the bower of the queen of the fairies."

Athena stopped still when she saw Frederick. She looked back at Aphrodite and attempted to hide her joy but her eyes filled with delight, and a soft smile curved her lips.

Frederick also attempted not to show his pleasure at the sight of his beloved, but he couldn't stop looking at her. He almost fell off the stage before he turned back to arrange a few pots of flowers.

Next to the stage stood Warwick, again watching the three of them. Aphrodite knew he couldn't help but notice Athena and Frederick while she acted as if her life were just as usual.

A puzzled scrutiny, then a quick glance at Aphrodite followed, but Warwick said nothing as he watched the attentions Frederick gave Athena throughout the afternoon, holding her arm, being careful that she did not slip, making sure she had a comfortable place to sit.

The rehearsal moved along quickly, although James insisted on using expansive gestures. Athena still knew only a word or phrase here and there and became confused even when holding her play book, but Frederick knew all of his lines and hers, and acted almost as if he were translating for her. All in all, it went as well as anyone, even Terpsi, could expect.

Warwick was not the only person who'd noticed the closeness of Athena and Frederick as well as Aphrodite's detachment. Terpsi noted them with interest and intense jealousy. Foolish, helpless little Athena always fell on her feet while fear filled Terpsi—fear she would never find anyone to love as she loved Callum, fear he would leave and she would be alone, fear she would grow old with Aphrodite, the two of them reminiscing about their salad days, raising ugly little dogs and growing fat.

She could not lose him.

"Callum!" Terpsi shouted in desperation. He started when he heard her voice and turned to run out of the ballroom.

"Callum," she said in a softer voice and added, "I am worried about our parts in act four. I would like to go over our lines again."

"I do not know why," Callum growled. "We know every word."

"There's one place I'm not sure about how I move around you. Please?" Terpsi begged.

Callum nodded, held the door for her, and followed her outside grumbling.

After they had repeated their lines perfectly, Callum threw the play book on a bench and started back toward the house. "I told you we need not practice again."

"Callum!" she shouted but he continued to move away.

The play will be finished tonight, Terpsi reflected. To-morrow is the ball. The next morning the house party will break up and I will never see Callum again.

He would return to Scotland, and she would go back to London where endless parties and Venetian breakfasts and routs and balls and evenings at Almack's and Vauxhall and Astley's awaited her, but they sounded boring and repetitious because Callum wouldn't be there. She would never again see his strong, beloved face or hear his voice with the slight burr or have him look at her—with approbation or with praise, it didn't matter. She just wanted him to look at her. Hadn't she been trying to get him to notice her for days?

"Callum! Please!" she shouted again before he had left the garden. This time he stopped.

"Why did you leave me?" she asked before she could stop herself, before she lost her nerve.

"What?" He turned and looked at her, confused.

"Why did you leave me? Why did you leave me?" she repeated to make sure he understood this time.

"I wasn't the one who left. Well, perhaps I did, but I didn't think my absence would be noticed." Callum studied her, his brow creased. "I thought you had lost interest in me, not that I could blame you."

"You thought I had lost interest in you? How ever did you come to such a caper-witted conclusion?" Terpsi took a few tentative steps toward Callum. After all, he hadn't left yet. Perhaps a bit of hope remained.

"When I last saw you, you were flirting with five men. I was the dull fellow watching." He turned and started up the steps.

"Callum, stop. Please come back." He paused and turned to look at her. "Didn't you understand? I did that so you would pay attention to me."

"What?" He stepped closer. "Are you mad?"

"I tried to make you jealous so you would come up to scratch."

He stared at her in disbelief. "You thought I would make an offer because you were flirting with other men?" He moved to stand only a few feet from her, studying her as if she were bacon-brained. As, perhaps, she was.

"I believed you would be more interested in me if other men found me attractive."

Callum said nothing but continued to frown.

"It was foolish, I know." Terpsi sighed and dropped onto a bench. "You should realize by now that is how we Herringtons think. That is why they call us the Mad Herringtons. But it worked for Artemis. That's how she got Sanderson to offer for her. You were so slow that I had to do something. I had been trying to get you to propose for weeks."

"Well, you see, I left the hunt for Lady Terpsichore because the other young men had so much more to offer. I could not understand what a lovely young woman like you could possibly want with a dull stick like me."

Terpsi studied Callum. He looked at her, his body leaned toward her. She knew this was the time for the truth. No more games, no more flirtations and larks.

"I love you," she said. "I loved you four years ago. I love you now. You broke my heart when you left. Please do not leave me again."

Callum's head jerked up. "You love me?"

"I have loved you for years, and I don't think you are a dull stick. I think you are the most wonderful man in the world. Please don't leave me again." Her voice had begun to tremble and she had to blink quickly to keep her tears from flowing down her cheeks.

A smile spread across his features as he moved toward her, lifted her from the bench, and took her in his arms. When he lowered his lips, he did not place a gentle, chaste kiss on hers but gave her a kiss filled with all the longing and emotion he had stored up within him. At least, that was how it felt to Terpsi, who returned it with all her yearning.

"My love, my bonnie love," he repeated when the kiss was completed. He leaned back to look at her and smiled again. "My love."

"And so, you will marry me?" he asked as he nuzzled her ear. "I believe it will be a good idea if we marry quickly."

"Callum, my love, such haste is unusual for you."

"My love, I have waited for four years. I do not wish to wait a moment longer. I will ask your father for your hand this afternoon." He kissed her again, then pulled away. "Unless that would not be proper. This house party is for Aphrodite to announce her engagement. Should we wait?"

"No, I don't want to wait." She looked up at Callum's face, smiling down at her. "And that's not just because I really do not want to wait. If you haven't noticed, this week will not lead to a marriage between Aphrodite and Frederick."

"No, I didn't realize that. You see, I was too busy watching you."

"You were? I thought you were busy not watching me."

"There wasn't a minute when I didn't see you, that I didn't know with whom you were flirting or the level of the necklines on those scandalous gowns you wear."

"Used to wear," she corrected.

"Ah, sweet Terpsi, even when I was not in England, I kept up with you. I read every bit of the London newspapers, looking for a hint of you, and I asked my friends for any news about you when they went to London, but somehow I missed out on the fact that you would be here or I wouldn't have come. I wouldn't have put myself through the pain another time."

Terpsi was so pleased with his words, she kissed him again.

"So, if I kept track of you from Scotland, how could I not notice you and Ridley here?"

"Why didn't you say anything?"

"What did I have to offer you? No more than I did when I left four years ago. You've always lived in London. You like excitement. What would you want with a dull stick like me, living hundreds of miles from London?"

"I will not have you saying that. You're not dull. You are loyal and responsible and kind. All the Herrington sisters are looking for someone stable and loyal and responsible—except Ditie, of course, although she has not realized that yet."

"And, I really do like to kiss you," she said. With that, Terspi lifted her lips to his.

She again nestled against his chest. "Oh, I am so happy. I knew I could never marry anyone but you."

"Certainly you would have. You were meant to have children to love, to be surrounded by your family."

"But I wanted only *your* children, Callum. If I couldn't marry you, I would have grown into a fubsy-faced termagant."

"Well, you may yet become a termagant, my love, but never fubsy-faced." He kissed her again to remind her that he loved her, sharp tongue and all.

"I must confess something," Terpsi began after a few delightful moments. "I will always love you. I will always adore you. But I am afraid that I will not always obey you."

Callum laughed until he had to wipe his eyes. "Oh, my darling shrew, I had not expected you would. However, if you could obey me occasionally, it would be pleasant."

"You do not mind that I will not be an obedient wife?"

"For four years, my friends and family have pushed docile young women at me. I could have married a woman who would obey me and make my life comfortable, but I wanted only you."

Overwhelmed and left speechless at these words of love, Terpsi lifted her lips for another kiss.

"But what will you find to do in Edinburgh?" he asked. "It is not London. I fear you will find it exceedingly dull."

"Not with you there."

"No, we need to talk about this now. What will you do in Edinburgh? I do not want you to discover you cannot live away from London. You must understand that I cannot live away from Scotland where my family and estate and business are."

"Certainly there are writers around Edinburgh. I have heard that Walter Scott lives close to town."

"Yes, he does."

"He knows other literary people, so, you see? I shall have a great deal to do. I shall begin a literary salon that shall be the envy of London."

"Oh, my bonnie love, of course you will."

Chapter Sixteen

In the excitement of the evening, with the drama only minutes away, Aphrodite could almost forget the mare's nest in which she found herself.

Terpsi, in a white Swiss muslin robe over a sea green slip, twisted in front of the mirror in an attempt to see the flowing curls Mignon was brushing.

"I didn't remember you planned to wear a slip under your costume," Aphrodite said.

"Callum doesn't like me to wear clothing made of flimsy, transparent material." Terpsi smiled abstractly into the looking glass and adjusted the lace fichu that covered her modestly.

"Oh?" Aphrodite stared at Terpsi. "And you agree with Callum about this?"

"Certainly. And, of course, Mama has asked me to dress more decorously," she added.

"You look lovely, both of you." Aphrodite smiled at her sisters. "Terpsi, I have a feeling you have a secret. Do you wish to tell us anything about you and, perhaps, Mr. Mc-Reynolds?"

175

"Oh, Terpsi, you sly boots. Tell us!" Athena coaxed.

"Perhaps later." Terpsi smiled again and tossed her hair so she could watch the curls bounce.

"Oh, my dears, you are lovely." Their mother swirled into the room, beautiful in a flowing gown of Russian flame with gold beads and a matching Moorish turban. The scent of frangipani floated about her. "Is it any wonder everyone says that the Herrington family has the most beautiful women in England?" With a smile, she settled back in a chair.

"Now, tell me, darlings, which play is this? Are they lost in the forest? Or is it mistaken identity? Or, perhaps, twins? I am afraid Mr. Shakespeare's plays confuse me."

"In this one, Mama, they are lost in the wood," Terpsi explained. "There are two sets of lovers, Hermia and Lysander—played by Athena and Mr. Horne—and Helena and Demetrius, who are Ditie and Warwick."

"Oh, I think I remember a little. Is there a magic spell?"

"Yes, Mama. Demetrius was in love with Helena, then he fell in love with Hermia and is engaged to her."

"And he says terrible things to Helena," Athena added. "But it's all right in the end, Mama."

"Yes," Terpsi said. "In the end, all the lovers are together: Athena and Frederick, Callum and I, Aphrodite and—" Terpsi stopped. The three looked at Aphrodite, who intently inspected her hairstyle. "Helena and Demetrius," Terpsi finished.

"Thank you, darlings," their mother said. "I always get those people confused. Why Shakespeare had to give both women names beginning with an *H*, I don't know. It is so difficult to remember which is which."

Aphrodite forbore to mention that Hazel had five children whose names began with an *A* and would have used the vowel for many more if their father had not requested that she use a few other letters of the alphabet for variety.

The marchioness rose. "You are all lovely, and I know we will enjoy your little play very well." She waved at her children and left.

Aski, in a green and gold costume with bells that jingled as he walked, joined his sisters in the hall. The four descended the backstairs to avoid being seen by the other guests of the house party and those from the neighborhood who had been invited to swell the audience. They found the other actors behind the lattice covered with vines and flowers that served as the back of the stage.

"Ah, fair Helena," Warwick greeted Aphrodite. "You are lovely."

"Thank you, Demetrius. You look very dramatic tonight."

Susannah had dressed the men in clothing that appeared more Elizabethan than Greek. The open neck of Warwick's shirt displayed a broad and very masculine chest. At the sight, Aphrodite's breath caught in her throat. Without the defense of her engagement, she felt vulnerable and extremely uncertain about how she should act toward a man who exuded such virility.

Fortunately, at that moment, Aphrodite's attention was caught by the obvious alarm of her little sister. Athena had looked around the corner of the stage, gasped, then hurried to Frederick. Until this week, Aphrodite thought with a sigh, her sister would've come to her with her fears, but their lives were changing at a pace she was finding difficult to keep up with.

"Oh, Frederick," Athena said to him. "I'm so frightened. There must be at least thirty people out there."

"More than that," Aski said. "Geoffrey counted fifty before he came back."

"Oh, dear." Athena sighed. "I will never remember my lines."

Frederick patted her shoulder. "I know every word you are to say. If you forget, I can whisper them to you."

"Certainly an original idea for actors, isn't it?" Warwick spoke from behind Aphrodite. "Fair Patience, do you not care that your fiancé is so attentive to your sister?"

Aphrodite turned to face him. "I'm pleased that my sister feels more comfortable now. I do not want her frightened while she's on the stage."

Warwick looked at her, his face inscrutable and his eyes filled with questions. Aphrodite turned away as she heard Terpsi welcome the guests. Then James stepped on the stage and said, "'Now, fair Hippolyta, our nuptial hour draws on apace.'" The play had begun.

In the years to come, Aphrodite marveled that she had survived the evening without bursting out in laughter or breaking down in tears far earlier than she finally did.

She also wondered how Mr. Shakespeare would have felt if he had seen Athena, terrified and unable to speak, silent as a beautiful statue in the middle of the stage. At first, Frederick whispered the lines to her, but, when it became obvious that she was too frightened to speak above a whisper, he maintained a dialogue with himself, shouting his own lines, then saying Athena's in a softer voice while she nodded her head or fluttered her hands. He ended each of her speeches with the explanation, "That's what Hermia said." The audience listened politely, even applauding his efforts.

"If I had had to act opposite your sister, I would have killed her," Warwick muttered. "It is well that my cousin is such a patient man."

As they played their parts as the feuding Oberon and Titania, Terpsi and Callum gazed at each other with such love that their hostility was hardly believable, but no one cared.

James, with his theatrical gestures, knocked one of the

fairies off the stage, but she landed on the soft lap of Mrs. Horne, who awakened for only a moment to shoo the unhurt girl away.

Aphrodite would have been delighted to see her family so happy if she hadn't gone through most of the play in a trance, distracted by the closeness of Warwick. She looked into his eyes when he spoke to her the lines of love written by Shakespeare. " 'The object and the pleasure of mine eye is only Helena.' " She almost believed him, then reminded herself this was only a line in a play. She was not Helena; he was not Demetrius.

The minutes hurried past until Callum ended the play with the lines, " 'So shall all the couples three ever true in loving be.' "

The cast bowed as the audience stood and clapped. Finally Callum silenced them with a gesture, led Terpsi toward the front of the stage, and nodded at Terpsi's father.

The marquis stood and inclined his head toward Mrs. Horne. "I thank our hostess for allowing me to share our happiness with our friends and family at her evening of entertainment." He stopped and held out his hand for Hazel to join him. "The marchioness and I are pleased to announce the engagement of our daughter Terpsichore to Callum McReynolds. We bless this union and welcome Mr. McReynolds to the family."

As Athena and Aphrodite rushed to their sister, Callum kissed Terpsi.

"Terpsi, I am so happy for you." Aphrodite gave her sister a hug before she turned to Callum. "And you look amazingly cheerful for a man who plans to spend the rest of his life with my sister."

"Oh, I know what I'm taking on, Aphrodite. I know she'll lead me a wild dance, but if she kisses me often enough and tells me she loves me every now and again, I believe I shall be able to put up with her." He looked at his beloved with such love Aphrodite could not doubt their future joy.

"There are refreshments laid out in the dining room," Frederick said. "Let us meet there to toast this happy union and those actors who performed for us tonight."

The crowd filled their plates, congratulated Terpsi and Callum, and told all the actors how well they had performed.

"You were wonderful, and you looked like a picture," the squire said to Aphrodite, lifting her spirits until she heard him say the same to Athena.

"My, you looked lovely," Susannah told Athena, who smiled happily while she held onto Frederick's arm.

"Just lovely," James agreed as Athena basked in their praise.

"The play was not so terrible, Frederick," Athena said. "Best of all, everyone says I looked lovely."

"As you always do," he agreed.

"Perhaps, Freddie," Athena said, "perhaps we could build a theatre in one of the gardens so we could have more plays."

Then Athena sat with Frederick next to his mother while Mrs. Horne shoveled in the food he brought her. Even the white toad displayed a tiny smile.

As she searched for someone to talk to, Aphrodite noted Aski in a corner. She wandered over to chat to him before she realized she would be interrupting a private conversation.

"The house party will be over tomorrow night, and Geoffrey and I will return to school," Aski told Elsie. "But you and I will see each other in a few years, when you are finally out. I promise I will dance with you and show you around town a bit."

Elsie touched her eyes with the handkerchief Aski handed her. "I will miss you."

Hugh Ridley escorted Gwendolyn to the supper table while Fothergill searched the room for a partner. When he saw Susannah's daughter, he sat next to her. All in all, the merry atmosphere of *A Midsummer Night's Dream* seemed to have entered every bit of the parlors.

In a far corner, Warwick sat with Susannah and James. Aphrodite tingled from the top of her braid to the tips of her toes, so aware was she of his scrutiny. Although he frowned occasionally at Athena and Frederick, most of the time he fixed her with the odd stare she had seen all day. What did it mean?

The marquis and marchioness held hands and walked through the throng of guests, speaking with each person, nodding graciously. But when her father nuzzled her mother on the neck, Aphrodite had all the joy and love she could handle for one evening. With a glance around to see if anyone were watching her, she came to the lowering conclusion that not a soul was. They were all too wrapped up each other. Even Warwick had turned to laugh with his sister.

Aphrodite inched toward the doors which led to the gardens. In a moment, she was outside.

At the bottom of the steps, she paused. Where should she go? The lake, she decided. The perfect place for a quiet time to think, to get away. She started toward the path to the lake, contemplating sitting in the little summer house to watch the reflection of the moon on the water, to try to come to some understanding of the hodgepodge of emotion that filled her: joy for her sisters, a large amount of uncertainty about her future, a tiny bit of loneliness, and another feeling she couldn't quite define about how their lives were changing. She felt a bit of disappointment but even more relief that no longer would Terpsi and Athena turn to her for help and advice.

No, she decided, sorrow that she would not be their

advice-dispensing sister was not the problem. Her sisters would never again come to her laughing and dancing to tell her about new beaux or ball gowns or any other things sisters shared. Instead they would become matrons, wives, and mothers, giving advice to their children. That was as it should be.

But what of her?

She paused at the bench that overlooked the lake and sat down. Perhaps this was far enough from the merrymakers for her to find peace. She smiled for a moment and thought of the times she'd spent here with Warwick in these last few days.

She banished the thought of him from her mind and forced herself to contemplate the future. Would she find a man she could respect and love? Would anyone love her or was she to grow old alone, the maiden aunt of her siblings' children? She shuddered.

"Are you cold?"

It was Warwick's voice but, for a moment, she didn't respond, assuming perhaps she had imagined him. Despite all her effort not to think of him, he did fill her mind.

"Are you cold?" he repeated.

Aphrodite turned. He stood behind her. Did he have that same odd look in his eyes that had been there all day? She could not tell in the darkness but rather guessed he did.

"I will give you my coat if you are." He began to shrug out of it.

"No, thank you. I am comfortable. I've been thinking."

"May I join you?"

Aphrodite slid to the end of the bench to give him room to sit, but he sat only an inch from her. He did not touch her, but she could feel his warmth.

"And your thoughts made you shiver?" he asked angrily. "I don't doubt that. How can you stand to see your fiancé dangling after your sister? Why don't you do something?

Why are you out here, leaving her to flirt with him? Go back inside and tell him to behave."

"I am not going to marry Frederick."

"You cried off?" He paused and seemed to consider her words. "When?" Warwick demanded.

"This morning, during our walk."

"Why didn't you tell me?" His voice echoed through the small clearing.

Aphrodite rose. "I did not see that it was your concern. I knew Athena loved him."

"You did not see how the fact that you are no longer to marry my cousin is any of my concern?" His shout cut off her words as he, too, stood. "Have I not been telling you all week that it is my concern?"

"Well, certainly, as the head of your family."

"No, I mean my concern. *My* concern. As a man." He strode around the small area in agitation. "Why do you think I have been following you around all day? I wanted to see if you had been hurt, if you needed a friend, if you were going to go through with this foolish marriage or if you had come to your senses. In case you needed, well, not necessarily a friend, but if you needed *me*." He struggled to gain control and turned to her. "Why didn't you tell me?"

"I thought it a matter between Frederick and myself. He loves Athena. I could not marry a man who loves my sister."

"Of course not, but you didn't tell me anything, any of the times I asked you. Certainly you could read my actions. Surely you could tell how worried I was that you would enter a loveless marriage with a man who doesn't deserve you, that you contemplated marrying a man who doesn't recognize your worth when I was there, all the time, waiting."

"Waiting? You were? Why?"

"Because I love you."

Stunned, Aphrodite moved away from him and leaned her back against the balustrade. Was the man mad? "What did you say?"

He moved to stand in front of her. "It cannot come as a surprise to know I love you. I have been as assiduous in my attentions as a man can be toward the woman who is to marry his cousin. Even my sister noticed that."

"You love me?" she asked. Daring to hope, she looked up at him. "You love *me*?"

"Yes, dammit, I love you."

His words were those she would have guessed Warwick would use to declare himself. "You are not playing with my heart again?"

"Two years ago, I was a fool. I found you very lovely even then. It frightened me. I was not ready for love and pretended my heart was whole, but it was not. I never forgot that kiss."

"I cannot understand why you would love me." Aphrodite shook her head. "I am not as beautiful and sophisticated as your usual flirts. I have seen you with the most gorgeous of high-fliers."

"I never fell in love with any of them."

"I am not even the most beautiful woman in my family."

"You have no idea, do you?" He took her hand and held it against his chest. "You really do not know that you are the most beautiful Herrington of all because you are filled with so much love—for your family, for everyone. Love shines out of you with a glow that makes you far more lovely than anyone else. I have often wished I could be enfolded in the warmth of that love."

He put his hand under her chin and tilted her head so she looked into his eyes. "You cannot doubt that I love you."

No, she could not doubt that he loved her. Everything

he had said and done during the house party convinced her of that. They had spent time together. He had shared her burdens. He had shown he preferred her over any other woman. His eyes spoke the truth. He did love her.

She had begun to form the words to tell him that she loved him when he pulled her into his arms and kissed her, a kiss filled with loving and longing, a kiss that awakened a hunger she had only guessed existed.

The kiss was nothing like the pecks Frederick had dropped on her cheek. Even the kiss Warwick had given her two years earlier paled beside this one.

Amazed at how marvelous this kiss was, she wound her arms around Warwick's neck and pressed her body into his. He put his hands on her back to pull her more firmly against him. And, shamelessly, she returned every touch, every movement with her own until, out of breath, he pulled back and looked down at her.

"Oh, my," she said, barely able to think.

"I was not sure," Warwick said. "I had hoped, but I did not know if the passion would be there." He smiled, then leaned down to kiss her again.

Then her mother's words exploded in her mind. Had she forgotten so soon? *She* was the responsible daughter. She was not her sisters. She was not a wanton. The thought stiffened her body. She unwound her arms from his neck and pushed him away, then tried to step back but hit the balustrade. "No, I cannot."

"You cannot?" He did not release her from his arms but looked at her, confused. "You cannot? But you have. You are."

"No." Her body leaned toward him, yearned to be held by him, but she moved away from the circle of his arms. "I cannot. You may have been misled by the behavior of my sisters."

Even to herself she sounded ridiculous. After having

delved into the depths of desire, she had become a Puritan, but she continued. "I am not criticizing them, you must understand. I love them, but perhaps their behavior has made you believe that I would behave loosely."

She glanced at Warwick. He wore a puzzled frown. "Perhaps," she attempted to explain more clearly, although she was not sure that she understood her reasoning herself. "Perhaps the fact that Athena stole my fiancé or that Terpsi flirted with Mr. Ridley while wearing her improper gowns led you to believe that I am the kind of woman who would break her engagement with one man only to kiss another in the moonlight mere hours later, but you are mistaken. I cannot," she repeated. "I am not like that." And, with those words, she whirled and ran toward the front door.

"But I want to marry you."

She stopped for a moment and looked back over her shoulder at him. To be the wife of this man was what she wanted more than anything in the world. Then what was wrong with her? Why could she not run to him and throw herself in his arms?

Because she could not. Because, for a moment she had given into what this man aroused in her, and it scared her to the depths of her being.

If she gave into her longing, she would no longer be herself. If she gave into desire, she would be no different from the rest of her family.

She whirled toward Warwick. "Do you believe that I am the sort of foolish, lustful woman who breaks her engagement to one man and then becomes engaged to another on the same day?"

"It's not the same day, my love. It must be after midnight by now."

"It is obvious you have no idea who I am, my lord." It was even more evident to Aphrodite that she was no longer certain of who she was. The small amount of logic she retained told her she could not answer Warwick until she understood who she was and the identity of the woman who came to life in his arms.

"I am not the type of woman who leaps from one man to another within only a few hours." She realized her voice was very loud and filled the clearing. With an effort, she spoke quietly but firmly. "I do not do that."

"Of course not. I didn't think that." He ran his hand through his hair. "I've mishandled this. Aphrodite, I've never told a woman I love her. I never thought I would. When I recognized I had fallen in love, you were almost engaged to my cousin."

Warwick took a step toward her but when she started toward the house, he stood still. "My love, I was so relieved when you told me you broke off the engagement with Frederick, I didn't think. I just acted. You must know I meant no dishonor."

"Thank you." To her horror, tears prickled in her eyes. What was wrong? She never cried. She blinked rapidly to try to stop them.

"I hoped you returned my love," he continued. "In fact, I am certain you do."

"I . . . I don't know. I cannot think right now. Please, I beg you, leave me alone." She had to get away now, before she started to cry, and Warwick pulled her into his arms again. "Please." Her voice cracked.

But she knew he would not. As she moved toward the house, he reached out a hand. "Please don't do this, Aphrodite."

It was not his fault, she knew. It was her problem. She was not brave enough to flout the rules that she had lived by all her life, in spite of—or possibly because of—her family. For so long, she had been so unlike the rest of her emotional family. How could she face society—no, that was not the consideration. How could she face *herself* if she were no longer the different daughter? The responsible one? After twenty years, could she throw her pride away in one night and become a true Mad Herrington?

She could not.

She refused to look at Warwick. She had hurt him, she knew she had, but he did not understand the war going on inside of her.

"Thank you for a nice evening," she said, always polite, as she dashed away from him, wiping her eyes with the back of her hand.

"You're not crying, are you, my love? I'm sorry. I never meant to make you cry."

In his haste, Warwick stumbled over something. She heard him hit the ground and swear. The fall gave her a moment to run ahead of him before he got to his feet. He was quickly up and after her, his feet pounding across the drive, then up the steps, but she reached the house ahead of him. She hurried inside, slammed the door and locked it before he could enter. When she leaned against the door to catch her breath, she could feel it vibrating with the blows from his fists.

"Aphrodite, let me in. Let me show you how much I love you. Let me tell you how sorry I am that I upset you. Please."

Her tears flowed freely now. Confound it! Why did she have to be good? Why could she not be a Mad Herrington, as harum-scarum as the rest of them? They were all happy, and she was miserable.

Why couldn't she just toss the door open and throw herself in Warwick's arms?

Because she could not do it, that was why. Because she was Aphrodite, the reliable daughter, the reasonable daughter, the passionless daughter, blast it! And she did not know any other way to act.

"I'm sorry, Aphrodite," he shouted. "Please open the door."

Instead she pushed herself away from the door and headed up the steps to cry herself to sleep.

Chapter Seventeen

"Ditie, what's the matter?" Athena asked.

Blinded by her tears, Aphrodite ran into her younger sister in the hall outside their rooms.

"You're crying, Ditie. What's the matter? You never cry." Athena followed her into the bedroom, in spite of Aphrodite's determined effort to close the door with her sister on the other side.

"Nothing, dear," Aphrodite said as she blew her nose on her tiny handkerchief and attempted to dry the tears that still streamed from her eyes. "Please leave me alone."

"Oh, no, Ditie. You never leave me alone when I'm unhappy. I came up here to get a shawl, but I am not going to leave you. Not now, not when you need me." A look of complete lack of comprehension covered Athena's face. "But you never cry, Ditie. I don't know how to make you feel better."

"I know, dear." Aphrodite threw herself on the bed and allowed the sobs to take over.

"Is it because of Frederick? Are you crying because you won't be marrying him?"

"No, darling." Aphrodite tried to smile so her sister would not be upset, but the tears wouldn't stop.

"Oh, Ditie." Athena patted her shoulder, then patted it again. "There, there, love." She continued the slow, gentle strokes but waited almost a minute before she said, "There, there," again.

When no lessening of the sobbing was apparent, Athena said, "Just a minute," and tiptoed out of the room, leaving Aphrodite to believe she could weep in solitude.

But, in only a moment, Athena returned, closing the door softly behind her. "See, Aski, Ditie is crying."

"She never cries," Aski whispered. "But she is," he added with wonder in his voice. He approached the bed and patted Aphrodite on the right shoulder while Athena went to the other side of the bed and patted the left. "There, there," he said. "There, there."

Torn between her own grief and the sight of her completely ineffectual but loving siblings' attempts to comfort her, Aphrodite didn't know whether to laugh or cry. Then she thought of not seeing Warwick, of not having him tease her, of not laughing with him. The idea of him no longer making her feel special and beautiful hurt so much she burst out into fresh sobs.

"Go get Terpsi," Athena ordered Aski. "She'll know what to do."

In a moment, the door opened and Terpsi entered.

"Ditie is crying," Athena pointed out. "There, there," she added to Aphrodite, who had struggled to sit up and wipe her face with the handkerchief Aski handed her.

Terpsi determined the problem with a glance. "Thank you, Aski and Athena. You go back to the party. I'll take care of her."

"Do not tell anyone, please," Aphrodite begged before she threw herself back on the bed.

Aphrodite heard the door close again, then Terpsi's hand was on her shoulder. "Come here. Sit up."

When Aphrodite sat up, Terpsi hauled her into her arms. "What's the matter?" Terpsi asked. "You never cry."

"Nothing," Aphrodite managed to say between sobs.

"Oh, I understand. You're crying because this has been such a wonderful week." Terpsi patted her sister on the back. For some reason, it felt much more comforting than the efforts of her other siblings.

"Yes. Wonderful. You're happy and Athena's happy and I'm happy for both of you." Aphrodite's voice quivered.

"But Athena has stolen your fiancé."

"Oh, no, that's not the reason I'm crying." Aphrodite looked into her sister's anxious face. "No, not at all. I believe Frederick is perfect for her. He and I would not have been nearly as happy."

"Then why are you crying?" When Aphrodite didn't answer, Terpsi guessed, "Warwick?"

Sobs overtook Aphrodite again. "Yes," she said with a tremor in her voice.

"Do you love him?"

"Oh, yes."

"Does he love you?" Terpsi rubbed her hand up and down Aphrodite's back.

"Yes."

"How do you know?"

"Because he helped when Aski was in trouble and because he looks at me in a way I don't really understand but I know what he means. And he's been kind."

"Warwick has been kind?"

"Oh, yes. And he laughs with me." Aphrodite paused to wipe her eyes. "And he said he loved me and wants to ma–ma–marry me." She wept into the sodden handkerchief again.

"Warwick wants to marry you? I didn't think the man

would ever fall in love. That is wonderful. Why are you crying?"

"Because this morning I was engaged, almost, to Frederick, and this evening Warwick asked me to marry him."

"What's wrong with that, Ditie?"

"I'm not like that, Terpsi," Aphrodite choked out between sobs. "You and Athena could handle having two fiancés in one day, but I don't do that sort of thing. And besides, I was . . . I was cuddling with Warwick." She buried her head in her hands.

"What's wrong with that?"

"Terpsi, I was shouting and crying and then I kissed him, passionately. I don't do that."

"But how was the kiss?"

"Oh, Terpsi!" She raised her head and looked at her sister. "It was w–w–wonderful." Then she broke into sobs again.

"Then what's wrong with wanting to kiss a man who wants to marry you? The man you love?"

"Because it is not at all like me. I'm becoming—" She stopped and dabbed at her eyes. "Oh, I hate to say this, because I love you, but I am afraid, oh, Terpsi, I am so afraid I'm becoming like you." Then she broke out in loud, hiccuping wails. "Terpsi, I'm passionate!"

"It is all right, Ditie. Really it is. Haven't you noticed that Athena and I are becoming more like you? We have both matured and become more responsible for ourselves and our lives. If you have become less sensible and more passionate, well, that's wonderful, too."

Aphrodite sniffed. It was true. Both her flighty sisters had decided to marry fine, unexceptionable men and were very happy about that. She had no fears that either would play their husbands false. No, they would have many children and grow old, content in the love of their spouses.

Perhaps she didn't have to be the responsible one the rest of her life. A smile forced its way through the tears.

"Do you think, Terpsi? Do you really think I could be happy married to Warwick? I never saw myself with someone like him. I thought I'd marry someone a little dull, like Frederick or . . ."

"Or Callum? Don't apologize. You see, I don't find Callum dull at all. Often, our hearts lead us where we would never have imagined."

"But, Terpsi, I cannot believe I've changed so much in such a short amount of time. I used to be so proper, but I've changed. The thought of not being with him hurts, terribly."

"You have to decide, Ditie. Do you think you could you be happy with Warwick?"

Could she be happy with Warwick? She'd never considered a life that was not of the utmost propriety, but it seemed foolish to cling to what suddenly seemed very outdated and staid precepts when kicking out of the traces, just a little, would make her so very happy.

But she couldn't do that, could she? Why not? she wondered. Look what being good had almost gotten her. Matilda Horne as a mother-in-law.

Could she stop worrying about her fears and all the propriety she had considered so important? Could she just allow herself to accept love? Could she finally realize that she was a passionate woman who desired Warwick as much as her mother desired her father? That she craved his kisses the way Athena used to crave the kiss of every man she saw?

She shivered with delight, and the tears stopped.

"Oh, yes, I could. I could be very happy with him." She kissed her sister on the cheek, gave her a radiant smile, and sat there, completely and thoroughly happy for a moment before she said, "Thank you, Terpsi, thank you."

"Wonderful!" Terpsi pulled her sister from the bed and

twirled her around. "We shall plan the most marvelous triple wedding."

Warwick stood outside the door Aphrodite had closed in his face.

She had locked him out. He cursed at himself. How could he have been so cow-handed? He had bungled the situation terribly. The reason was obvious. He had never been in love before, never told a woman he loved her and meant it, never asked a woman to marry him. He obviously didn't have a knack for it.

Of course she was cautious. After she'd just terminated one engagement, he'd tried to force her into another. He doubted even Terpsi could handle being engaged to two men in one day, much less his Aphrodite.

His Aphrodite, he thought with what he knew must be a fatuous grin. He knew she was his, but she wasn't so sure. He had to prove he was trustworthy. He must proceed slowly and diligently. Let her see how courteously and cautiously he courted her, how assiduous and sincere his intentions were.

He could not rush his fences this time.

He shook the door again, but it was still firmly locked. Where was the footman? How could he get into the house? He heard the noise of the party in the parlors so he descended the steps to go around the side of the house.

The moon had gone behind clouds and there were no lights in the front windows. He felt his way to the garden steps. Once inside the house, he passed quickly through the parlors and nodded to those who attempted to congratulate him on his part in the play. His goal was to reach his chambers to plan.

"My love," he vowed. "I will win you yet, and I will make you very happy. I promise."

* * *

The next morning, Aphrodite woke up late, her head aching from tears but filled with hope for the future. She rang for breakfast and for Mignon, then looked out her window.

Goodness, it was later than she'd thought. Her siblings were dressed and outside already. On a garden bench sat Terpsi and Callum. He held her hand and she smiled up at him, her face glowing with happiness. Aski and Elsie played hide-and-seek in the maze while Athena and Frederick strolled along the driveway. Frederick placed his hand on Athena's shoulder when they stopped to chat, and she looked at him adoringly.

They were so happy, those Mad Herringtons.

Then she remembered the reason her siblings were up and about. They had all promised to help Susannah clear away the clutter in the ballroom and put away all the costumes. Perhaps she would see Warwick there. Then she could explain. She could tell him she loved him and would marry him. She wasn't sure how, but certainly she would think of something when she saw him.

After breakfast she dashed down the stairs like a hoyden. Not like Aphrodite Herrington at all, she reflected with a grin. When she ran into the ballroom, she discovered her siblings, the other actors, and a dozen servants just finishing the tidying up.

Aphrodite finally found Warwick coming from behind the stage, carrying the lattice with James. Like many of the men, he wore a comfortable tweed coat and beige pantaloons, but he looked far more handsome than the others. Suddenly feeling very shy, Aphrodite watched Warwick stand the lattice against a wall and wipe his hands.

"Here's my robe," Aphrodite said as she walked across the ballroom.

Warwick looked at her, his eyes calm and almost without expression. Was there just a little twinkle there? She couldn't tell. Was he thinking he had made a terrible mistake?

"Thank you, Aphrodite," he said as he took it and handed it to his sister.

"Ready, Thomas?" Frederick shouted from the terrace.

"Thomas, are you leaving?" Aphrodite asked, reaching for his arm.

"Frederick tells us there is a mill not far from here. All the men are going. I cannot disappoint him." Warwick started away, then turned and came back. "I hope to see you at the ball tonight. Please save me a dance."

"Certainly."

He nodded and walked away.

"That did not look promising," Terpsi observed.

"I could hardly drag him away from what Fredrick arranged, but I will do something," Aphrodite said.

That evening, Aphrodite had Mignon take special care with her toilette. She wore a gown of grass-green gossamer over a slip of embroidered white crepe with a matching fichu and her mother's pearls. Mignon had styled her hair with a braid high in the back and short curls framing her face. Carefully, Mignon placed a grass-green bandeau on her head.

"I don't believe I've ever seen you lovelier, Lady Aphrodite," Mignon said.

"My dear," her mother said as she entered her daughter's room, "you are in excellent looks this evening." She settled herself on a sofa. "Please forgive me for not coming to see you earlier, but your father didn't tell me until after my naps about his discussion with Frederick—about the broken engagement and Frederick's desire to talk to him about Athena when we return home. Now, sit down, and tell me everything."

"Oh, Mama, there is nothing to tell. Frederick fell in love

with Athena, and she with him. I couldn't marry the man
my sister loves." She pulled on her long white gloves and
clasped a bracelet around her wrist.

"But I thought you and he were so much alike. Both
so . . ."

"Responsible," Aphrodite supplied. "I truly believe he is
the best man Athena could have chosen. We are all too
aware of her unfortunate tendencies."

"Oh, yes, my dear." Hazel placed a hand against her
chest.

"Athena told me she would never kiss anyone else because it would hurt Frederick."

"Then you must be right, as usual, my responsible
daughter."

Oh, she wished she could say, *"I do not want to be that
daughter anymore! Tonight I am going to seduce a man."*
But all she said was, "Yes, Mama."

"How do you feel, my dear?" Her mother took her hand.
"It cannot be easy to break your engagement when your
future seemed settled."

"I am fine, Mama."

Dinner was served to the house party and a few neighbors. Warwick had been seated next to Terpsi while Aphrodite sat at Callum's side. A more transformed Terpsi
Aphrodite couldn't imagine. She chatted with Warwick but
kept her eye on Callum, who smiled back at her, although
he was a polite dinner partner to his future sister-in-law.
Warwick was a perfectly charming dinner partner to Terpsi;
occasionally, but only for a moment each time, he smiled
at Aphrodite. There was no way for Aphrodite to draw his
attention. She considered flirting outrageously but she had
not changed enough for that.

After dinner, the ladies adjourned to their chambers to
refresh themselves before the ball began. Aphrodite sent
Mignon to help Athena and Terpsi and studied herself in

the looking glass. As she put a finger on the fading furrow between her eyes, she knew she had to do something about Warwick herself. Now. She would not ask Terpsi's advice or discuss this with their mother. She would approach Warwick tonight.

She looked at herself again. Staring back at her was the Aphrodite Herrington she had known for years: staid, responsible. Pretty, yes, but oh-so-very proper.

She removed her bracelet then slowly stripped her gloves off, rolling them down her arms, before pulling them off each finger and, finally, the thumb. She tossed them on the dressing table. As she scrutinized herself in the looking-glass, Aphrodite lifted her arms and removed the bandeau that crushed her curls, then pulled out each hairpin, throwing them on the dressing table. When her hair was loose, she shook it and ran her fingers through it until it flowed riotously down her back.

She glanced at the lace fichu in the front of her dress and considered removing that. No, she thought. She was, after all, Aphrodite Herrington and still *somewhat* proper.

Once more, she inspected herself. The furrow between her eyes had disappeared.

She would marry Warwick—and she would be glad to put that in the betting books at White's—or she wasn't a Mad Herrington.

Twenty couples had joined in a country dance when Aphrodite entered the ballroom. From the top of the staircase, she searched for Warwick among the deep blue of the gentlemen's jackets but she could not find him. Callum twirled a smiling Terpsi in the center of the floor, while next to the French windows Frederick brought Athena a cup of lemonade. In the light of a hundred candles, Aphrodite could catch a glimpse of her parents dancing the country dance with a passion unique to them. On the platform, a small orchestra was finishing the last notes of the dance.

She strolled down the stairs, looking over the banister for Warwick. Where was the man when she needed him? When she wanted him? Her eyes searched the crowd.

Then she found him. He had not joined the just-completed country dance. Instead, he stood with Hugh Ridley and Fothergill, talking and drinking champagne.

With a satisfied smile, Aphrodite stood at the bottom of the steps and watched him.

"Hello, Ditie," said Aski who had crossed the floor to greet her. "You look different."

"Tell the orchestra to play a waltz next," she said.

"Ditie, I don't think Mrs. Horne permits waltzes here."

"Tell the orchestra to play a waltz now!" she commanded, then gave Aski a look that had him hurrying away to do her bidding.

Aphrodite firmly set her sights on Warwick. Although he had his back to her as he chatted with Fothergill, she moved across the room toward him with her hips swaying as she had seen her mother and sisters do so often.

All the guests turned to watch her as she crossed the floor. She heard her mother and sisters call her name but ignored them. Her goal lay straight ahead.

Fothergill's mouth fell open when he saw her. Wondering what had caused his friend to stare, Warwick turned his head, then spun around to watch her slow and sinuous progression across the floor. She looked at him from eyes she hoped were filled with invitation.

Warwick dropped his glass. It shattered when it hit the floor, but he didn't notice.

She sauntered closer and noticed his eyes had filled with delight. When she finally stood in front of him, Aphrodite shook her head so the curls whirled around her shoulders.

Then the small orchestra began to play a waltz.

"Thomas?" she said, her voice low and seductive. "Thomas, I believe this is my dance."

A broad smile crossed his features. In answer, he took her hand and led her to the floor before he drew her into his arms.

"I hope, my love, that this means you will marry me," Warwick said as they whirled around the ballroom, alone for a few moments until the other Herringtons joined them.

"Of course I will. I love you." As they waltzed, Aphrodite walked her fingers up Warwick's neck and through his thick hair.

"People are watching, my love."

"Let them watch." Aphrodite laughed. "I am, after all, a Herrington, a Mad Herrington." She put her other hand behind Warwick's neck and pulled his lips to hers.

Perrine, Jane Myers.
The mad Herringtons

APR 2003